ROOKIES

ROOKIES
GAY EROTIC FICTION

WITHDRAWN

EDITED BY
SHANE ALLISON

CLEiS
PRESS

Published in the United States by Cleis Press, Inc., 2246 Sixth Street, Berkeley, California 94710.

Printed in the United States.
Cover design: Scott Idleman/Blink
Cover photograph: Andersen Ross/Getty Images
Text design: Frank Wiedemann

First Edition.
10 9 8 7 6 5 4 3 2 1

Trade paper ISBN: 978-1-62778-029-2
E-book ISBN: 978-1-62778-046-9

Contents

INTRODUCTION: PROTECT AND SERVICE ME

So I'm driving at a breakneck speed to get home to watch the last thirty minutes of my favorite TV show, *The Vampire Diaries*, when I see to the right of me a cop car sitting idle on the soft shoulder of the highway. I slow down, but I'm too late. The cop behind the wheel pulls behind me and flashes those red, white and blues that strobe in my rear window. I figure he probably had me on his speedometer half a mile back because I sure as hell wasn't paying any attention to how fast I was driving. I pull over into the parking lot of some old abandoned store outlet and kill the engine. This cop saddles right up behind, his lights practically blinding me. I think of the two-hundred-dollar ticket he's about to issue, how I can't afford that on my part-time job salary. I know what he's going to ask for, but I don't make a move. These trigger-happy cops in this town will riddle you with bullets and ask questions later.

I put both hands on the steering wheel like they tell them to do on my favorite reality TV show, *Rookies*. I hear him walking toward me, and then a fat white beam from his flashlight peers in on my neck. He tells me, "Good evening." This cop sounds nice enough. I don't make any sudden moves. He asks me if I know how fast I was going. I don't have a clue, so I pull a number out of my ass: forty miles per hour. He corrects me by telling me that I was going sixty in a forty-five. I'm thinking how totally screwed I am. He asks for my driver's license, registration and proof of insurance, in that order. I reach slowly inside my left pocket and pull out my wallet. I hand him my license. Had he stopped me a week before, I would have found myself being carried off to jail for driving with a suspended license. I had to pay through the nose to get everything reinstated, all over outstanding speeding and parking tickets.

As I hand him everything he asks for, I glance up at him. He's a tall drink of water, a brawny, football-player-build type of black man with voluptuous lips and short hair faded to the side. He tells me to hang tight. I'm checking him out as he walks back to the patrol car. This man's got an ass I could eat for days and still have leftovers. Suddenly, I'm not thinking about some show I'm missing, but imagining this cop booty-ass naked, and I'm betting that he's got nine, maybe ten inches swinging between those muscular thighs. This is the kind of scene I sometimes fantasize about: being pulled over by some smoking-hot rookie policeman, to be cuffed and then fucked into submission, yet those kinds of tawdry scenarios only happen in gay porn videos. A queer can dream can't he?

I will do anything to get out of this ticket, even resort to servicing some big thick cop dick. He finally returns with my license and everything else and says he's going to let me off with a warning. Luck is with me tonight. I thank him in the most cordial, sweet voice I can muster. I glance at his crotch in hopes of seeing a bulge tenting those blue cop-pants, but there's nothing. I wouldn't object to him slinging his dick in my face, but like I said, that kind of thing only happens in gay porno flicks.

I missed *The Vampire Diaries,* but I didn't give a shit about vampires when I had dick and bubble cop-ass on the brain, conjuring up the idea for the anthology you now hold in your hands. I had wanted to do a spin-off of my bestselling, critically acclaimed *Hot Cops* for quite some time, so why not something about rookies? The scribes I have assembled here have risen to the occasion, giving the best gay erotica featuring rookie policemen their dirty minds could conjure up. Among the talented writers you'll find here are: Rob Rosen, Logan Zachary, Gregory L. Norris, Bearmuffin, Landon Dixon, Michael Bracken and a plethora of new gay erotic tastemakers. I hope you get just as much pleasure out of reading these stories as I have.

Shane Allison
Tallahassee, Florida

COCKS AND ROBBERS

Rob Rosen

It was my first week on the job and damn if I didn't have the rookie blues. Mainly because the station was a lot like a fraternity house, all the grunt work falling to me, the lowly pledge, as it were. Meaning, every bit of dreary paperwork came flowing my way, same for interviewing the dredges of humanity, too, not to mention most of the nonessential errands, like picking up lunch for the sergeant.

This is how I ended up at the out-of-the-way sandwich shop, solo, my partner back at the station waiting for me to return with his lunch as well.

Only, suffice it to say, they had a mighty long wait ahead of them.

Long enough for me to shoot my load that is.

"Hello?" I said, after I entered the tiny eatery, the few stools vacant, cash register oddly unattended. "Hello?" I repeated when I got no response, which suddenly sent a spark of alarm up my spine, and my hand instinctively reaching for my Taser gun, which is all they allowed the rookies to carry.

And then I silently stepped inside before making my way to the kitchen door, my heart beating out a mad samba in my chest as a trickle of sweat tickled its way down my face. I cupped my hand to the door and pressed my ear up. Two guys were talking, one a bit louder than the other, and, by the sound of it, in a rather threatening manner.

In other words, good cop that I am, or one day hope to be, I was inside in a flash.

"Freeze!" I shouted, Taser held up between rather shaky hands.

Except the bad guy didn't freeze. Guy on the floor did, but that was because he was already tied up. The other one, the one stuffing the cash in his front pocket, took off like a rocket, whizzing by me and out the back door.

"Fuck," I spat, giving chase when I should've been radioing for help. Only that would've given the guy a head start. And, yes, rookie blues frequently equate with rookie stupidity, but fuck if I was gonna let my first perp escape with a pocketful of cash.

The thief was fast, too, hurtling down the back alleyway, arms pumping at his sides. Me, I'd just finished cop training and was in the best shape of my life, so he might've been fast, but he wasn't getting too far ahead of me. Not that it mattered, really, seeing as he zigged when he should've zagged, running straight into a dead end.

"Freeze!" I repeated, hands steadier this go around as he tripped, fell and landed with a thud against the Dumpster to his side. This time he froze. Thank goodness. Because by then I was having a hard enough time catching my breath. Same for him as he lay there staring up at me, arms scuffed, dirtied, mouth in a snarl as his chest rapidly rose and fell.

"I only got a stack of singles, dude," he coughed out as he

pushed himself up on his elbows and leaned against the Dumpster, rubbing his scraped-up arm.

I moved in a few feet, taking him in. Dude was my age at best, slighter by far, nice looking, scruffy and with eyes so blue as to put the sky to shame. His T-shirt had ripped during the fall, revealing a single dense pec and a pert pink nipple. His jeans had a gash in the knee and a tear in the crotch, which, of course, is where my eyes landed last. See, he was going commando, the hole big enough to see in, balls and shaft cast in shadow. I gulped as I gripped the Taser.

"I'm taking you in," I croaked out.

He grinned. "Yeah, I can see that."

I shook my head and aimed my weapon at his exposed chest. "To the station."

His grin widened as he tossed a wink in for good measure. "C'mon, it was barely twenty bucks. Give a guy a break." He moved his hand to his jeans, fingers digging inside the frayed denim as he yanked out his cock. "I can play nice if you can." The wink made its triumphant reappearance.

I blinked, the sweat stinging my eyes, which were fairly bulging by then. Them and my cock both. This they didn't teach at the academy. "Get up," I squeaked out.

He tugged his prick. "I'm working on it."

I shook my head. "That's not what I meant."

He pointed at the obvious bulge in my cop trousers. "You sure about that?"

In fact, I wasn't sure about anything right about then. Because, like he said, it was twenty bucks. And twenty bucks wasn't worth the time it would take me to write this whole mess up. Not to mention, I certainly wasn't following rookie protocol when I gave chase without backup. Plus, as his prick grew and grew, my cop resolve shrunk. Go figure.

"Hands behind your back," I told him, my voice suddenly thick as molasses.

He nodded and pushed himself up onto his knees before standing up, swollen cock sticking out of the hole in his jeans, swaying as he caught his balance, the plum-sized head glistening in the sunlight. Then he did as I'd asked, hands behind his back.

I nodded and again aimed the Taser his way. "Now up against the Dumpster."

His nodding continued as he turned and moved in that direction, face against the Dumpster, hands still behind his back. I sighed, exhaled, and grabbed for my standard-issue cuffs. They got slapped on without a fuss. Still, he grumbled, "It was only twenty bucks, Officer."

I kicked at his feet and spread his legs apart, then held his head in place as I reached around into his front pocket to retrieve the evidence. "Twenty-three," I corrected him, after counting it all. "Looks like you picked the wrong dump to rob."

He chuckled. "Tell me about it." Then he turned his head to the side. "But then I wouldn't have had the pleasure of your acquaintance."

I moved in closer, my front to his back, cock pressed up tight to his ass. "Always this smart-mouthed when you're handcuffed and pressed up tight to a Dumpster?"

The chuckle repeated. "Well, when you put it that way…"

I reached my hand around and grabbed his prick, which surprisingly hadn't shrunk even an inch. "Just shut the fuck up," I rasped, giving it a stroke as he shuddered and moaned, the sound reverberating through my chest. "You'll have to be punished for what you did, you know."

He nodded and pushed his ass into my crotch. "Yes, sir, Officer."

Man, how those words made my prick throb. And it was then that I spotted the milk crate, and the punishment I had in mind was made all the easier to come by. Emphasis on the come.

I grabbed his tattered shirt and moved him to the side of the Dumpster, even more out of sight should someone head down our narrow stretch of alleyway. Then I grabbed the crate and plunked my ass down, all before I grabbed his belt and pulled him in, that thick dick of his so close I could smell the sweat and musk off of him. Then I undid the belt strap and yanked his jeans down to his sneakers. Seconds later, he was lying across my lap, arms still cuffed behind his back, alabaster ass exposed to do with as I pleased. And, yes, I fucking pleased.

Up my hand went, then down, hard, harder again, palm meeting flesh until a swatch of red rose up from behind the spread of white. He groaned with each progressive spank. As did I. "No." Smack. "More." Smack. "Stealing." Smack.

"Yes, sir," he yelped, his steely cock smashed between my thighs.

Again my cock throbbed at the words. "You don't sound convincing," I said, before spitting into my hand, the same hand that quickly found his tight, little asshole. "Maybe the punishment shouldn't have been only skin-deep." A slicked-up digit wormed its way down and in, far, farther still, until it was buried completely inside of him. He moaned again as he pushed his ass up to meet my hand, and moaned even louder as a second finger, then a third, joined the fray. "You shoot your load on my slacks and that Taser gets triggered."

He grunted and nodded. "Yes, sir."

Pulse went my throbbing prick. "Better," I said, thrusting my fingers into his deepest recesses.

His moaning and groaning soon swirled around my head

like a swarm of hornets before he admitted, "But, fuck, I'm close, sir."

In fact, I, too, was pretty damned well ready to explode. And so I retracted my fingers and tossed him off my lap. "On your knees," I told him, releasing my cock from its tight constraints as I watched him huff and puff and eventually right himself, dick dripping as it pointed up at me, those eyes of blue again laser-locked with mine.

I stared from them to the exposed nipple to his rigid prick, jacking away as I repeated the visual loop, until my knees started to buckle and my balls began to tighten. It was then that I finally moved, standing over him as he stared up at me. Lightning fast, my fist made quick work, until my head shot back and the loudest moan yet spewed out, echoing off the brick walls that surrounded us.

And then I came. And came. And came some more. All of it landing in one dull *splat* after the next on his dirtied and torn shirt before dripping down in great big gobs of white. I shook the last remaining aromatic drop out and slapped my prick against his cheek. "Lesson learned?" I asked as menacingly as possible.

He nodded, though I seriously had my doubts. In any case, I uncuffed him, stuffed my shrinking prick back inside my slacks and watched as he hawked some spit down on his rod before grabbing an eager hold. It didn't take long, either. Guy's eyes were rolling back a minute later, back arched as he aimed and fired, sending out one giant stream of come that landed a couple of feet away before pooling on the cement.

When he popped his eyes back open, I was again greeted by those magnificent orbs of blue. He grinned and winked and put his hand up to his heart. "Scout's honor," he panted. "No more robberies."

I returned the grin in kind. "You ever were a Boy Scout?"

The hand got moved away. "Nope."

I turned and headed out of the alleyway, hollering over my shoulder, "Next time it's gonna be Tasers first, ask questions later."

"It's a date, Officer," he yelled back.

I grinned and then headed back to the sandwich shop, where the same guy I'd left was still tied up. "Oh, sorry," I apologized, quickly cutting the ropes with a handy and rather sharp nearby knife. Then I handed him the twenty-three bucks. "But I did at least get your money back."

He smiled widely as he rubbed the spot where the ropes had once been. "You chased that guy just for this?"

Among other things, I thought, squelching the blush that was trying to worm its way across my face. "All in a day's work."

The smile rose on his face. "My hero," he practically purred, my rookie blues in an instant wiped clear the hell away. "Sandwiches are on me, next time."

"Is now too soon?" I quickly asked, wondering what I'd tell the sergeant when he asked where I'd been all this time.

He moved an inch closer, then an inch closer still. Nice-looking guy, too. Brown eyes like liquid chocolate. "No time like the present, Officer," he replied, one hand suddenly on my chest, the other considerably lower down.

Fuck the sergeant, I thought, with a barely stifled groan, closing the gap with a tender kiss. *I'll think of something, good cop that I am. Or someday will be.*

BUSTED

Johnny Murdoc

I leave my car sitting in the McDonald's parking lot. It won't start. It won't do anything. I could call home, but instead I walk. Between work and home, there's a park, and there's something in my pocket that will make the day better.

It's June, and it's warm. The air is dense. It doesn't take long for me to sweat. Summer in the Midwest: it's not the heat that does you in. It's the humidity. A thick cloud of water hangs in the air. The whir of crickets, and cars passing by sound like they're swimming to you. It's almost midnight, but it's only cooled down a little. The humidity holds the temperature like a heated blanket. I peel my work shirt up and over my head, wearing only my white tank top beneath it.

I walk until the streetlights thin out, and the night sky becomes apparent. Small businesses give way to houses, which give way to trailers. I cross a set of railroad tracks. I remember being a kid, walking down the line, balancing on the steel rails, listening for oncoming trains, feeling their deep rumble vibrate through my bones, until I could see them. I never played chicken with a train. Like my Dad always said, you don't fuck with some things.

Not too far past the tracks, past the firehouse, there's a park. The small plot is fairly isolated, surrounded by a chain-link fence on three sides and two abandoned houses on the other side. One lone streetlight casts a yellow net over the small collection of jungle gyms and merry-go-rounds. Someone's bad idea of a skate park sits off to the side, a poorly constructed collection of wooden ramps and a repurposed handrail. A lone skater rides back and forth across the simple setup. It's late, but I figure he has his own problems. And I can respect that. I nod at him as I walk by. He nods back.

I make my way to the merry-go-round on the far side of the park. It's been there all my life. The rust-red paint is peeling off, exposing prior paint jobs and, in places, the bare metal beneath. Ten years ago, some parents got together to get it removed, after a girl broke her arm while playing on it. Other parents defended it. There was a town hall meeting. This little merry-go-round has been through a lot.

I sit down on the edge of it, and it creaks beneath my weight. I lie back and look up to the stars. The streetlight is just far enough away that I can actually see some of them. Beneath them, I feel small and insignificant.

I reach into my pocket and pull out a lone plastic-wrapped joint. It's wrapped to keep it safe from the smells of burger grease, French fries and sweat. I unroll the plastic, hastily plucked from the kitchen drawer as I ran out of the house this afternoon, and shove it back into my pocket. I free my lighter from my other pocket, and sit up to light the joint. I cup my hand around the flame out of habit even though the air is still and unmoving. I inhale deeply.

I don't know if it's actually the weed or only my imagination, but I relax quickly. I use my feet to give the merry-go-round a little shove, setting myself on a slow spin. The stars begin to dance above my head. Behind me, beside me, around me I can still hear the skater riding his board. The grind of his wheels on the plywood ramp creates a steady rhythm that helps set me in a groove. *Shucka-shucka. Shucka-shucka.* I take a drag from the joint. The red tip of it glows like a star in the night.

Slowly, everything falls away, until it's just me, the merry-go-round and the stars. Nothing else. No worries. No job. No car. No parents. No money problems. Nothing.

The sound of skateboarding starts to fade, one long *shucka* as he skates away.

I take another drag, and my dick starts to get hard in my pants. When I was younger, I started coming down to the park to get high and jerk off. I could lie here for hours, staring at the stars and stroking my dick. Now I get hard any time I get down here, like a Pavlovian response to the cold metal, the weed and the stars.

I tuck my hand into my waistband and grab my dick, and consider masturbating for old time's sake.

A siren cuts through the air, one brief, piercing tone, like an exclamation point in the night. I pull my hand free from my dick and sit up quickly, digging my heels into the gravel to stop the merry-go-round. It takes my vision a moment longer to stop spinning, but even then I can't help but miss the flashing red and blue lights.

Goddamn.

The officer's already out of his car, holding a flashlight in my face. He steps close to me. "Don't you think you should at least try to hide that?" he asks, pointing. I look down at my hand: I'm still holding the joint.

"Goddamn it," I say. I don't even think about trying to run. The officer drops his light, and I can see him better. He's young, younger than you expect a cop to be, barely older than I am. He's close to me. I don't even think I could hop over the back fence if I tried. My dad's going to fucking kill me. If work finds out, I'll lose my job.

The officer steps closer, reaching his hand out. His badge reads SHARPE.

"Hand it over," he says. I extinguish the joint on the merry-go-round, and hold it up for him. He takes it out of my hand. "Come on," he says, "get in the car."

"I'm sorry, sir, it's just..." I feel like a kid again, sitting in the principal's office.

"Come on, get up. You're going for a ride." He puts his hands on his hips, to make his point.

"If you knew the kind of day I'm having," I say. I stand up, and realize that my dick is still kind of half-hard. I hope the officer doesn't notice. He puts a hand on my arm, and it's softer than I expect it to be and his skin is warm against my bare arm. He walks me over to the car.

"Come on, get in," he says, opening the back door. He holds my head at an angle so I don't hit it as I slide into the backseat. He closes the door and walks around to the driver side. I slide down into the seat. He gets in and gives me a look in the rear-view mirror. I can't read him. My erection is completely gone.

He puts the car into gear, and flips a switch on the dash-board that makes the red and blue lights disappear. He pulls out onto the road and makes a right turn.

What the fuck? I think. The police station is the other way.

The road inclines and we make our way up a hill. I'm vaguely familiar with where we are, but I don't have a clue as to where we're going. He keeps driving until the houses drop almost entirely away and we're surrounded by trees. I had a friend that lived in this area when I was younger, but I haven't been up here in years.

I think about asking him where we're going, but as confused as I am about that, my mind is moving a mile a minute thinking about what's going to happen to me when my parents find out that I've been arrested for smoking pot. What my brother's going to think when he finds out. Growing up, I remember my older brother being a perpetual fuck-up, but then he went to war. Now he's become the golden boy. His picture sits on the mantle above the fireplace. He's wearing his dress blues and smiling. There are no pictures of me in the living room.

The car stops, and I realize that I no longer have any fucking clue where I am. Or what's going on. The cop turns off the engine and gets out. He walks around to my side and opens my door.

"Come on, get out," he says.

"What?"

"Just get out."

I do as he says. We're high up. He's pulled the car up to a small opening in the trees, right at the edge of the cliff. Below us, I can see the entire city.

"Look, kid," he says, stepping up beside me. It sounds ridiculous, coming from him. "I know what it's like to have a shit day, okay?" I look at him, wondering where this is going. "I know what it's like to want to unwind, to get high and forget about everything."

"What—" I start.

"But doing it in the park isn't the best idea. Cops drive by there all the time looking for kids up to no good." He turns around, and walks back toward the car. For a moment, I think he's going to leave me behind. He sits down in the driver's seat, and through the light coming off his dashboard, I can tell that he's digging for something under the passenger seat. He finds it, I guess. He gets back out of the car.

"Up here," he says. "The cops never come up here. I don't think any of them know about it." He holds up a small baggie. It's filled with weed, and a small box of papers. "I took it off a kid, earlier. I hate doing that shit, but he was trying to get high sitting outside of the Gas Mart. I didn't have much option, with the owner standing over my shoulder."

I stand there, looking at him, completely unsure of what to do.

"Come on," he says. "You're not the only one who's had a bad day. Do you want to get high, or not?"

With that, he sits on the hood of the cop car and opens the baggie. He starts to roll a joint. It's not the first time he's done it. "Do you still have your lighter on you?" he asks. I reach into my pocket and pull out a cheap red lighter from the Gas Mart. I hand it over to him. He lights the joint and inhales deeply. He holds his breath and then exhales a cloud of smoke. He holds the joint in my direction. I give up, and I sit next to him on the hood of the car, take a drag, and look down over the city. The hood of the car is warm, almost too hot, beneath my ass.

"Damn," he says. He slides back off of the hood of the car and unclips his walkie-talkie from his shoulder. He starts to unbutton his shirt.

"What?" I ask.

"I don't want my shirt to smell like pot."

I try to get a good look at him without being obvious about it. Goddamn he's beautiful. His jaw is square and already showing a day's growth. His hair is short and black. It's hard to tell what color his eyes are. Beneath his blue cop shirt he's wearing a white cotton T-shirt that hugs his chest tightly. He

unbuckles his belt and takes off all of his gear. He steps around
the car and drops his shirt, belt and gun into the backseat.

He joins me back on the hood of the car. "I'm Cody," he says.

"Curtis," I say.

"It's nice to meet you, Curtis."

"You look awfully young to be a cop," I say.

He laughs. "I just graduated last year," he says.

"Where'd you go?"

"Over at Jeffco," he says, talking about the community
college.

"You from around here?" I ask.

"Yeah. Born and raised."

"Shit, you probably knew my brother, then. Bobby Rayes?"

"You're Bobby Rayes's little brother?"

"Born and raised."

"Shit, I got high with Bobby a few times. I'm surprised he
never told you about this spot."

"He went into the Army right after graduation."

"Yeah? What's he up to now?"

"He's in Afghanistan."

"No shit?"

"No shit."

He takes another deep drag on the joint. He leans back,
propping his elbows on the hood of the car. A plane flies above
us, its blinking light cutting between the stars like a flickering
comet.

"I keep thinking this has been the worst fucking day. Then
I think about one of Bobby's emails, about how fucking hot it
is over there. About how one of his buddies took a bullet in the
neck—"

"Jesus Christ."

"About how little kids try to sell him cigarettes, and he buys them because they're cheap. He buys cigarettes from ten-year-olds, and he's the good son. I think about all of those fucking things, and then I hate myself for thinking I've had a bad day because some kid vomited in the ball pit."

"Where do you work?"

"McDonald's."

"Fuck, that sucks."

"Yeah."

Cody passes me the joint. His face is blank except his eyebrows are peaked just a little, almost like he cares. I pass the joint back.

"I had to arrest some jackass for animal abuse today. His neighbors called us. Guy kicked the dog right in front of me. I used to have a dog just like it." Cody inhales. "Nobody got shot in the neck, though."

"I miss Bobby. Then I think about him shooting at people in cars and I hate this whole fucking country." I think that last part's one step too far, maybe Cody's going to get pissed and go off on me.

He looks down at his watch. "It's past midnight. It's officially tomorrow, so your bad day is over."

I look down at the joint in my hand, and realize that it's pretty much done for. I flick it off into the woods.

"I'm sitting on the hood of a cop car; I just smoked a joint with a cop. At this point, I don't know what the fuck kind of day this is."

Cody laughs. His laughter escalates until he's practically cackling. I can't help but laugh, too. Cody curls until he's almost sitting up, then he collapses back onto the hood of the car. His laughter trails off. "Oh, shit," he says. His chest is heaving. He looks straight up, watching the stars. His shirt is pulled tight across his chest, and it's pulled up a little, exposing a band of skin and the dark hair that disappears into his pants. His black slacks are tight across his crotch and his dick is easy to make out. Too easy, like it's almost hard or something. It lies across his hip, pointing in my direction. It's big. I blush and feel a little prickle as my nipples harden. My cock surges.

Cody laughs again, almost to himself.

"What?" I ask, looking away from him quickly.

"I was just thinking about—" Laughter cuts through his words. "I used to come up here by myself and jerk off. God, I haven't done that in years." His hand traces lazily over his chest and ends at his nipple, his finger flickering briefly over the pointy tip. "Fuck, I'm high."

The air feels different, a little bit wetter. I breathe in, breathe out. My heart is thundering in my chest. "I used to jerk off in the park."

"Yeah?"

"Yeah. My parents never cared when I walked to the park, so at night it was easier to hang out there and get high. Pot always makes me a little horny and there's nothing like jerking off outdoors."

"I know just what you mean." He lifts his other hand up and places it directly on his crotch. It's not an obvious move, almost an unconscious one. His finger traces lightly over the outline of his dick like it did over his chest a moment before.

"If I was alone—" he starts. His hand tightens on his dick.

I lie back. "My brother sent me this other email. I would have never thought he'd talk about something like this, but he was telling me about how guys over there jerk off together, sometimes. Like, there's no privacy, so—"

"Ha, ha," Cody laughs.

"He told me a couple of guys will jerk off in the Humvees on long drives. Like, they'll get hard from the vibrations on these hour-long treks, and some of them whip it out right there. Or at night, or long shifts, sometimes they have to lie there in their bunks, listening to each other jerk off."

"That actually sounds kind of hot."

"Yeah."

Another plane lazily crosses the sky.

"So, I don't want to weird you out or anything, but I could seriously go for a wank right now."

I laugh. "No shit?"

"No shit. It's been a long time since I did that up here. You think that'd be all right?"

"Actually, that sounds kind of cool."

"Sweet."

He doesn't waste time. He unzips his pants and pulls his fly open. I can see the bulge of his cock beneath his plaid boxer shorts. My angle's not perfect, but I can see enough. I unzip my own fly. Above me, the stars seem to spin a little, like I'm back on the merry-go-round.

Cody frees his cock, pulling it through the fly of his boxers. His cock is fat and long. He holds it so that it stands straight up. He looks at me and smiles. I blush. My own dick is impossibly hard. I unsnap my fly and push my pants down a little until my dick pops free, landing on my stomach.

"Nice," Cody says. He's stroking his cock. His left hand traces a path slowly up and down his chest, trailing a circle around his nipple. His right hand moves slowly up and down his cock, savoring the strokes.

I lift my own dick up. It's not as big as Cody's, but it's big enough. No one has ever complained. I wrap my left hand around it.

"You left-handed?"

"Yeah—"

"I was just wondering. I had a friend who used to use his left hand, even though he was right-handed. Said it was like someone else's hand."

I'm not worried about it feeling like someone else's hand, I'm worried about watching someone else's dick. Cody's dick. I try not to be too obvious. I can't figure out what this is to Cody. I don't want him to think I'm gay, which is ridiculous. I'm sitting on the hood of a car with him, jerking my dick. This is pretty gay. I'm pretty gay. He initiated it, but it still feels like the moment could easily disappear.

"Relax," Cody says, his free hand landing on my thigh. I jump. He gives it a quick squeeze and then his hand drops away. His right hand is moving faster, sliding up and down his cock. The head glistens like it's wet. I see a bead of precum collect at the very tip and then Cody changes his stroke, letting his hand roll over the head of his cock, smearing the precum around. He lets out a little grunt.

My dick is hard and sensitive. I stroke it slowly, wanting the moment to last, knowing that if I go as fast as I usually do, this will all be over too quickly. I want to stay here all night, lying next to Cody, watching him jerk off.

Cody slips his free hand into the fly of his boxers and pulls his nuts out. His balls are huge and hang low, almost slipping between his legs. I lift my right arm and put it behind my head so that I have a little better view. Cody's eyes are closed. He's biting his bottom lip.

Cody pulls up his shirt, exposing his fit, hairy chest. He pulls it up high enough that his nipples, dark and pointy, are exposed. He rubs his hand through the hair that trails from his pecs down into the waistline of his boxer shorts. It's intense watching him pleasure himself, knowing that he's hitting all of his own right spots.

"Fuck," he says.

The word, just whispered, makes my dick surge. His voice is deep and lost.

Cody pinches his nipple. The head of his cock flares, expanding. He looks close. I increase my own stroking speed. Cody thrusts his hips a little off of the car's hood, humping against his own hand.

I pull my right arm down and let it fall between us. I'm tempted to reach out and touch his leg. So tempted.

Cody's entire cock is slick with precum now. It sparkles in the moonlight. His hand makes wet slapping sounds as he strokes faster and faster. I don't know how much longer I can watch him. I get close to cumming and I squeeze my dick, trying to suppress my orgasm. My dick throbs, pulsing with my heartbeat.

Cody slaps his stomach lightly and then presses down on the area right above his cock, where his pubic hair is hidden by his boxers. He grunts like he's talking to himself. He lets his hand fall and his knuckles brush against mine. His skin is so warm. His hand moves quickly. I think he's going to pull it away but instead he wraps it around mine, threading his fingers through mine. Holding my hand, squeezing. This moment right here, this is why I was born left-handed. I can feel the motion of his entire body as he jacks off. It's too much. I cum. My toes spread out in my shoes and I can't help but grunt. Cody squeezes my hand again and the first shot of cum erupts out of my dick.

"Hell yeah," Cody says and he squeezes my hand even harder. His cock flares, it looks impossibly thick, and cum pours thickly and slowly out. My own ejaculate arcs up and out, landing on my shirt. One shot makes it past my shoulder and I hear it land on the car hood next to my ear. Where my cum comes out in quick shots, Cody's pours out, covering his hand and sliding down his wrist until it drips onto his side. He coats his cock with cum as he continues to stroke, his cum thick and bright white even out here in the dark. Cody groans, one long sound escaping through his teeth. His grip on my hand is impossibly tight, his arm muscle bulging. His chest contracts, the muscles on his chest defining drastically. His groan fades into laughter, the same deep laughter from earlier, right after we finished the joint.

"Damn, that was fucking great," Cody says.

My cock is starting to deflate and hangs against my fingers. Cody's cock is still rock hard. He jiggles it a little. It wobbles but stays erect.

"I forgot how good that felt, doing that here," Cody says.

He's right, it did feel good, but I'm not sure if it's the location or the fact that a beautiful man just jacked off sitting right next to me. Cody strokes his cock a few more times, his cum pooling between his thumb and forefinger until it slides over and drips off, half onto his stomach and half onto the waistband of his boxers.

"We made a fucking mess," he says.

I laugh and sit up. My dick lolls against my thigh and I pull my tank top up and over my head. I use it to wipe my hands clean.

"Mind if I use that?" Cody says. I hand it to him and he uses it to mop the cum up off of his side. He wraps it around his cock and cleans himself off. He holds the shirt up. "Think we should toss this?"

"No," I say. Hoping I didn't say it too eagerly. I reach out for it. It's soaking wet and reeks of cum. "I'll take it home and wash it." I'm never washing that shirt again.

Cody smiles. "This was nice," he says.

"Yeah."

Cody looks out over the city. I think about all of those

people, the rednecks and the assholes, and I think about how none of them know what happened up here tonight. I'm not sure that I do.

"Well," Cody says, slapping his legs. "I guess I should get you home or something."

I don't want the evening to end but I say, "Okay."

Cody slides off of the car's hood. He tucks his cock back into his boxers and tucks his shirt back into his waistband. I do the same. I wad my tank top into a ball.

"You got another shirt to wear?" Cody asks.

"Yeah. I got my work shirt."

I reach into the backseat and grab my shirt. Cody stands next to me and pulls his cop shirt out of the passenger seat.

"Where do you live?" he asks.

"Over on Parthenon." I start to climb into the backseat.

"You can sit up here," he says, gesturing at the passenger seat.

"Oh."

Cody smiles again.

The ride home is a quiet one. I speak only to tell Cody which house is mine.

"Thanks for the ride," I say, and open the passenger door.

Cody reaches out and puts his hand on my arm. "Hey," he says. "We should hang out again."

"Uh—sure. That could be cool."

"What are you doing tomorrow night? You work?"

"No. I'm off tomorrow."

"You want to go bowling?"

"Sure."

"Cool," Cody says. His hand leaves my arm and hops up to the back of my head. He runs his hand quickly through my hair in the back, kind of scratching. Petting.

"Tonight was fun. Don't let shit get you down so much. You're a good guy, Curtis Rayes."

"Thanks," I say, unsure of what else to add. Then it hits me. My car is still sitting across town. Dead. "My car, it—"

"I can pick you up here, if you like. Eight?"

"Sure."

"Cool. See you tomorrow."

"Yeah. See you tomorrow."

OFFICER JIM

Bearmuffin

Anybody will post just about anything on the Internet including cell phone videos and pictures of themselves having hot sex. Of course gay guys are no exception, and it's not surprising that that's how Officer Jim Hanson found about the hot tearoom action in the Arts Building toilet on the campus of the University of San Diego.

Officer Jim worked as a campus cop at the University of San Diego. He had no experience, but he'd been in the Marines and that was good enough background for the job or at least that's what the employment department thought, so he was hired on the spot.

He was bisexual but with a decided preference for cock so you could say he was one of the growing number of straight allies who were partial to giving gays their civil rights.

Officer Jim was hung like a horse, uncut, and drop-dead handsome with big brown eyes framed by straight eyebrows. His mouth was inviting. Large brown nipples capped sweetly

toned pecs. Officer Jim had a boyish adorableness that attracted
the most jaded of studs. With a buzz cut, a chiseled jaw and
bulging muscles, he cut quite an imposing figure in his tight-
fitting uniform that boldly enhanced his youthful muscularity.

One of Officer Jim's duties was to surf the Internet for post-
ings about hot gay action among the college students. He found
plenty of information about places to suck and fuck all over
town, but Facebook was where he discovered pictures and
movies of hot young college studs sucking and fucking in the
dorms. Really hot pix, including some cum-shot close-ups and
even pix of guys rimming other dudes.

Now what went on in the dorms was not Officer Jim's business, but the hot action in the Arts Building certainly was. And
he found out that the toilet was one of the hottest places to find
some good suck-and-fuck action.

Of course no names were mentioned on the Facebook posting,
but the pictures were good and clear and it was most certainly
happening in some men's restroom somewhere on campus. Jim
was certain he would recognize any of these hot studs should he
ever run into them.

Well, Officer Jim took his sweet time investigating all the
toilets one by one. He almost gave up hope until one evening
when he hit the jackpot. He checked out Facebook again and
read a post that said, *Arts Bldg. Suck me dry, Friday, noon.*

Now the toilet stalls were pretty big, big enough to accom-
modate two or even three dudes and there were two big glory
holes between the last three stalls. You never failed to find a
hot young stud looking for some action. So Officer Jim was not
surprised when he came upon Rick Hernandez servicing Steve
Harris.

Rick was a tall, handsome stud with a fantastic body and a
big cock. He was a wrestler and his jet-black hair emphasized

his stunning green eyes. His angular features, full lips, enormous hard rod and spectacular low-danglers made him a real looker.

Rick was in the last stall, and Steve was blowing him through the hole. Steve was a football quarterback. Officer Jim heard the slurping sounds of cocksucking, so he went to investigate. When they heard his footsteps, Rick and Steve immediately stopped in mid-blow job.

Officer Jim was trembling with a strange combination of fear and arousal. He didn't know what to do. Should he arrest them or stay and join in the action, or leave? But his natural curiosity was piqued, along with his now-hardening dick.

Besides, there were no cameras in the toilet and unless somebody had snapped a picture of him with their cell phone nobody would be the wiser. He was a natural-born risk taker, and he figured there wasn't much chance of that happening—so he thought, *What the fuck, why not?*

He certainly had no intention of spoiling anybody's fun and he was no Nazi storm trooper. So he quickly went to the stall next to Steve. He pulled down his pants, sat down and started to beat off.

A few seconds later, Officer Jim noticed Steve peeking under his stall. Steve was a real beauty with a tight ass, big dick and fat balls. He had lips you could kiss all day. He stood six foot two and had wavy, dirty-blond hair and crystal-blue eyes. He was wearing a red baseball cap backward, a formfitting polo shirt and faded jeans.

Officer Jim felt a hand land on his calf. Steve whispered eagerly, "Stick it under and I'll suck it for you."

Officer Jim knelt down on the concrete floor and pushed his knees and lower abdomen under the partition so that his cock was now under the stall. Soon, he felt a hot mouth wrapping around his rock-hard cock. It felt so fucking good! It was so fucking incredible! Officer Jim had never been sucked by a dude in a toilet before!

Steve's mouth slid up and down Officer Jim's fuck-pole. Officer Jim could feel Steve's tongue eagerly licking the under-side of his cock. Officer Jim started to moan. Steve kept sucking Officer Jim, long and hard, taking in all ten inches of his long, hard cock. Officer Jim couldn't believe what was happening.

"Fuck, man, I'm gonna cum!" Officer Jim whispered under his breath. Steve kept sucking. Officer Jim started to shake and he blew his load right into Steve's gasping mouth. Steve just kept on sucking and swallowing Officer Jim's spurting cum. It tasted so fucking good!

After that totally mind-boggling experience, Officer Jim couldn't help going back to the hole. He knew there would always be someone willing to suck his dick. He wondered about Rick though. He'd never figured him to be a homo. Even so, getting your cock sucked by another testosterone-packed butch stud was exciting. Officer Jim couldn't wait for more.

The next evening, Officer Jim checked out the hole. He pulled out his cock and smiled as he watched his piss flow from his big pisshole and splash into the urinal. All of a sudden, Officer Jim heard this heavy grunt followed by a steady, smooth pumping sound coming from one of the stalls.

Officer Jim finished pissing and went to see who was back there. As he got closer, the moans and grunts got louder. He went in the adjoining stall and sat on the toilet. He noticed the glory hole had been stuffed with toilet paper. He poked it out and looked through the hole.

Officer Jim couldn't believe his eyes! Rick was in the next stall and Troy Benson, a tight end, was fucking him.

Troy was very handsome, with a sharply clipped goatee and a terrific smile. He was extremely muscular, with hefty, well-defined pecs. His biceps were magnificent, his belly flat, his legs powerful. His big, fat cock was long and always hard, his balls pendulous and full.

Troy was moaning and grunting lustily as he fucked the holy shit out of a bucking and swaying Rick, who was holding on to the toilet seat. Troy's jockstrap was pulled down to his knees and Officer Jim could see his muscular butt gyrating wildly as he plowed his cock up Rick's sweaty asshole. Officer Jim's eyes were glued to Troy's bucking ass, and his cock was getting harder by the minute.

Troy had the kind of full ripe jock butt you wanted to ram your cock into and fuck for a couple of hours. After what seemed like hours of endless fucking, Troy finally shot his hot wad up Rick's ass.

"Holy goddamn, fuck!" Officer Jim cried out when he saw all the cum dribbling out of Rick's hole.

Rick looked through the hole and saw Officer Jim. "Hey, dude," he whispered. "Wanna join us?"

"Fuck yeah!" Officer Jim said.

Officer Jim was horny as hell. His asshole was twitching with anticipation. He desperately wanted Troy's hot cock up his asshole. Officer Jim noticed that there was plenty of room next to the stalls for a good, long fuck.

Rick smiled. He was glad to see Officer Jim again. If he played his cards right, Officer Jim just might turn out to be a great fuckbuddy.

The three studs stood by the urinal. Rick was ogling Officer Jim who was just staring at Troy. His eyes were taking in every hot inch of Troy's superbly muscled body: the huge pecs, the superb washboard abs, the thick, pulsing cock.

Troy was just as eager to fuck. "Yeah, c'mon! Let's fuck, dude!" he said.

Officer Jim reached down and gave his bulging crotch a squeeze.

"Fucking A, dude," Officer Jim said.

Troy's cock jutted out lewdly. Officer Jim's eyes bulged at the sight of Troy's thick, uncut pecker bobbing in front of him. Once again, his eyes roamed over Troy's spectacular torso.

"Goddamn! You got a fucking hot body, dude," Officer Jim said.

Troy loved compliments so he began to flex. He raised an arm and exposed the golden silky tufts of hair swirling inside his armpit.

Officer Jim nuzzled his face into the thick hairs that swirled inside Troy's hot, musky armpits. He wrapped his fist around his spasming cock and jacked it hard as he lapped at the musky hairs. When Officer Jim looked down between Troy's legs, he saw that he was getting a fucking hard-on, too. Officer Jim moaned loudly, enjoying licking Troy's raunchy armpits.

Troy groaned. "Like that smell, don'tcha?"

Officer Jim agreed. The powerful male aroma was intoxicating.

Officer Jim's muscular ass was exposed, so Rick bent down and slowly circled his tongue around the hot puckered ridges of the policeman's hole.

"Yeah, fucking A!" Troy said. "Suck his fucking ass!"

So Rick began eating out Officer Jim's wonderful ass.

Officer Jim finished licking Troy's armpits, and now he was running his tongue all over Troy's pumped-up pecs. He took one of Troy's thick nipples and sucked it in between his lips.

"Fuck, yeah!" Troy grunted. "Suck those nips, dude!"

Troy grabbed Officer Jim's head and held him steady while Officer Jim chewed on his protruding nipples. Then he guided Officer Jim's head down along his sweaty, furrowed abs. He made Officer Jim stoop lower so he could kiss and lick the wash-board ripples of his muscular belly until he finally got Officer Jim's face down to his groin.

Troy thrust his cock and balls against Officer Jim's bobbing face. He was filling Officer Jim's nose with the powerful stench of his sweaty body. Officer Jim's probing tongue slurped noisily at the jock's fragrant crotch. Officer Jim was really getting down now. He mashed his face into Troy's musk-filled pubes and worked his tongue up and around his big thighs. He licked the sweat off of Troy's big balls and then landed his hot tongue on Troy's huge cock.

Rick continued to rim Officer Jim's beautiful ass.

Officer Jim zigzagged his butthole over Rick's fluttering tongue, thoroughly enjoying Rick's ass worship. Troy thrilled at the sight of Rick chowing down on Officer Jim's butt. Soon, Troy's butthole began to twitch. He wanted a rim job, too, so he spun around and stuck his butt right in Officer Jim's face.

Troy reached around and spread his cheeks as he butted his big hairy ass against Officer Jim's bobbing face. His hole opened wider and Officer Jim's flickering tongue slipped inside. Officer Jim's cute, boyish face was smothered in hot, musky wrestler butt.

"Yeah! Fuck!" Troy howled, wiggling his butt against Officer Jim's flickering tongue while he fisted his own hot, spasming cock. "Eat my butt, dude! Get that tongue up my hole!"

Officer Jim gripped Troy's sweaty boulder-like asscheeks and tore them apart so he could jam his wiggling tongue all the way up Troy's twitching bunghole.

Troy groaned loudly, grabbing on to the sink for support as he shoved his butt into Officer Jim's ass-eating face. "Suck my ass, dude," he barked. "Eat it, yeah!"

Officer Jim sucked harder, licking and rimming until the

wrestler's butt was slick and shiny with hot, frothing spit. Rick was eating Officer Jim's butt and Officer Jim was sucking on Troy's asshole. They jerked and heaved as the studs rimmed each other like there was no tomorrow.

"Okay, stud, you eat my cock now," Troy hissed at Officer Jim.

Troy turned around to face Officer Jim.

Troy cupped his hands behind Officer Jim's head as his cock quivered violently. The knob-like tip of Troy's precum-oozing cock hovered just an inch away from Officer Jim's trembling lips. Officer Jim's eyes glittered when he saw the piss-slit yawn and a drop of precum slowly trickle out. Officer Jim stuck his tongue out and brushed it against Troy's oozing piss-slit as the salty drop oozed on his licker.

"Yeah," Troy moaned. "Lick it. Stick out that tongue. I want ya to get a real good taste of my dick 'cause I'm gonna shove it up your fucking hole!"

Officer Jim's face was buried in Troy's groin. His nose and lips were lost in the thick musky nest of pubes. When Troy hunched forward his big sweaty balls slapped against Officer Jim's chin.

Hot, foaming spit drooled out of the corners of Officer Jim's mouth as he sucked in his cheeks and slurped on Troy's cock. It was spasming wildly between the tight end's legs and thick drops of precum began to ooze out of his pisshole.

Officer Jim ran his hands up and down the jock's golden thighs and slipped his fingers in between the crack of his sweaty buttocks. When he wiggled his forefinger inside Troy's hot and sweaty bunghole and churned it around, Troy went berserk.

"Aww, fuck!" he cried. Troy tossed his head from side to side; his muscles trembled. His eyes glowered as he rammed his cock all the way down Officer Jim's cock sucking throat.

"C'mon punk," he yelled. "Eat that cock. Yeah, I'm gonna fuck your face!"

Troy slam-dunked his mighty cock in and out of Officer Jim's mouth until Officer Jim's eyes began to water, and his throat got scratched and raw. His heart was pounding. Troy was choking Officer Jim with his magnificently veined cock.

Suddenly, Troy wrenched his cock from Officer Jim's mouth.

"Bend over, dude!" Troy barked, slapping Officer Jim's buttocks. "I'm gonna doink ya!"

Officer Jim's cock was flopping up and down, so Rick dropped to his knees and began to suck on the cop's irresistible meat.

"Okay, dude! Tory rasped, fisting his anxious meat. "Let's see that butt!"

As Rick sucked on Officer Jim's big, fat cock, Troy grabbed Officer Jim's firm buttcheeks and wrenched them wide open. Officer Jim's puckered hole was jutting out. It looked like two big lips waiting to suck around a big, fat dick. When Troy nudged the blunt tip of his cock against Officer Jim's puckered bunghole, Officer Jim started to squirm.

"Open up, dude," Troy hissed. He spanked Officer Jim's juicy butt until it was cherry red.

"You're gettin' this cock all the way up that fucking ass of yours, dude."

Troy grabbed his cock by the root and inserted it between Officer Jim's trembling buttocks. He grunted as Officer Jim's hole opened wide and allowed Troy's purple knob to slip inside.

"Yeah, fucking A!" Officer Jim cried. "Fuck me, stud. Fuck me!"

Troy's cock plowed up Officer Jim's bunghole. Officer Jim

broke out in a cold sweat. "Ah, fuck!" he screamed. His body went rigid for a split second. Troy got a firm hold around Officer Jim's waist and with a hearty grunt he rammed hard into him. Officer Jim's slimy bunghole suddenly snapped and gave way as Troy sunk his bloated cock in to the hilt.

Troy enjoyed the sensation of Officer Jim's ass canal sucking around his meat, drawing it deeper and deeper inside his butt. Rick jacked his cock as he continued to suck on Officer Jim's cock. Officer Jim was delirious with lust, completely and totally in the throes of hot homo passion. He was ready to blow his wad.

Troy's hot muscles shuddered, his mouth open and frothing. Hot streams of funky sweat ran down his magnificent muscles. His hot pulsing cock was just about to shoot its spunk.

"I got a hot load for ya, dude," Troy grunted.

Officer Jim was delirious. "Gimme that load!" he shouted.

Troy panted. He looked down at Rick, whose mouth was filled with Officer Jim's hot, sweaty cock. Officer Jim was about to spooge.

"Swallow my load!" Officer Jim barked. Troy heard Rick's stifled groans when Officer Jim's cock exploded and hot squirts of semen gushed down his gurgling throat.

Troy leaned forward and gripped Officer Jim tightly around the waist and slammed into him. Officer Jim's tight hole clenched around the root of Troy's spasming cock as huge jets of sperm squirted out of his cock and hurtled up Officer Jim's asshole.

Rick groaned. Any minute now he was sure to shoot his spunk.

Rick took his cock and aimed it right at Officer Jim's rippled stomach. A heavy fuck-spasm shook Rick's entire body as his cock erupted and he squirted several funky wads all over Officer Jim's heart-stopping abs. Rick's cum splashed on Officer

Jim's stomach muscles and dribbled onto Officer Jim's cock and balls.

Troy zipped up his jeans.

"See ya," Troy said. His dazzling smile exposed his pearly whites.

"Same time, okay?" Rick said.

"Fucking A!" Troy said, as he scampered out.

Rick's sturdy hands flew around his cock, jacking it to full-fledged hardness. He glared at Officer Jim, his eyes filled with lust.

"Wanna blow me?"

Rick grabbed his cock and squeezed it hard. Five inches of hot and hard throbbing meat pulsed lustily past his fist.

Officer Jim grinned and fell to his knees. He swallowed Rick's throbbing ten-incher. It sank balls-deep down his cock-sucking throat.

Rick cupped his hands around the back of Officer Jim's bobbing head.

"Suck that cock! Suck it!" Rick said.

Officer Jim did as he was told. He sucked and sucked until Jim's thighs trembled signaling his coming orgasm, and come he did, pumping and squirting one hot cum load after another down Officer Jim's cocksucking throat.

It was a rousing finish to a great session of hot sucking and fucking. Fortunately, his picture never appeared on the Internet and so he was able to continue to service the hot studs on campus without any fear of exposure until he finally quit his job—which happened about two years ago, when he went on to bigger and much better things.

HE COULD
STOP TRAFFIC

Gavin Atlas

O fficer Karl Wilkes tore his eyes off the college boy to check his phone. The incoming call was one he'd been antici-pating for weeks. He looked back up. The boy was Latino, and at second glance, damn familiar. His tight tan T-shirt show-cased a pumped chest and narrow waist. His shorts revealed tawny, muscular legs with a fine down.

Stop staring and answer the phone.

How did he know him? The boy's walk was sultry and confident. His muscular body reflected a disciplined workout. Despite the conservative haircut and textbooks, the boy seemed out of place. It could have simply been the sensuality rolling off him, but something made Karl think he belonged on a stripper pole, not on his way to class.

Answer the damn call, Karl.

As he clicked the TALK button, Karl saw the stoplight tattoo on the boy's neck. Heat curled through him as vague memo-ries formed. *Oh, hell. I think I've had him.* If he was who Karl thought he was, he was *Hondureño,* unbelievably good sex, and his name began with a *T.* What was it?

"Uh...this is Wilkes. Lieutenant, I'm about to give that presentation about the profiling program. Do I need to scrub it?"

Lieutenant Corley may have been lousy at returning calls, but he wasn't a prick. "No, that's important. Just make sure you have your Plan A ready for Main Street at five this afternoon."

Karl's eyes went wide. "Wait, I've been asking about this for months. Why—"

"Wilkes, a federal wig's son vanished last night, here in Houston. We're almost certain it's *El Sistema.*"

"Oh...fucking shit."

"Exactly. Disaster. On the other hand, the problem you've been going on about finally has everyone's attention."

Karl had apprised the department that the occasional disappearance of male prostitutes outside of a couple hustler bars was likely a larger operation that didn't just affect the "deviant" element. The white shirts at Main Street sometimes paid attention when gangs kidnapped women, but gay boys? Never. If any of them besides Corley had given a rat's ass before today, Karl wouldn't have known. "But do we have the...device? And two detectives?"

"Checking on the first question and one, but not two. Weren't you going to work on that?"

Karl huffed. "I've been scouring the region for agents who fit the requirements, but there's nothing. Now if I'd been chosen for the Vice Unit, I'd have prioritized—"

"Christ, Wilkes, trust me. I know what this means to you. You'll be on the unit once you've had a couple years under your belt. Everything you got by five tonight, clear?"

"Get back to me about the device, please, Lieutenant,"

Wilkes said, before his superior hung up. The hallway had cleared. Which room was C219?

He heard his cousin's voice coming from down the hall. "Officer Wilkes from the Houston Police Department was supposed to be—"

"Made it, Tanya." Karl jogged into the brightly lit classroom. He saw her wince, likely because he'd forgotten to call her "Professor Dawes" in the classroom again. But he had a recovery plan, and he turned to the students. "Just because she's my cousin doesn't mean she wouldn't have my head if I missed...this."

There was the boy, and he clearly recognized Karl. The name came to him. Tomás. Tomás Torres, the alleged pizza delivery boy who was really a stripper, who was really a nude housecleaner, who, so it would seem, was really a college student. Karl gave him a quick smile and turned away, blood rushing to his groin as his mind now flooded with memories: Tomás in nothing but a jockstrap taking Karl's dick in position after position. It hadn't been much more than a year. Had he gotten that swept up in work? How could he have forgotten how good it felt to be inside that stud? And how much fun they'd had afterward, talking, cuddling, and laughing at stupid movies? *Stop it. You have a presentation to give.*

He cleared his throat and looked at his cousin. Her face was a mixture of bemusement and mirth, but it was clear she was waiting on him.

"So, uh, most of you are in this class because you're about done with what West Harris Community College offers in criminal justice. Right? After graduation, many of you will be considering the police academy, but for those looking to transfer to Houston Central University, the geographic profiling program is something the city is very proud of. As a graduate—"

"When are the police going to realize that profiling is wrong?" The voice from the back of the room was loud, accusatory. Karl looked up. White male. Approximately twenty years of age. About five-eleven. Thin frame. Ratty tie-dyed T-shirt. Brown curly hair.

"Uh, geographic profiling is—"

"*You* of all people should know what it does to minorities! But you're blinded by the power of your badge."

Karl arched an eyebrow. "First, young man. Why *me* of all people?" He knew he looked black, and nine days out of ten if someone asked him how he felt about something as a "black man" he didn't blink. But he was also part German, Mexican and Navajo. If some clueless kid was going to lecture him on the prejudice of appearance, he'd better—

"Alan, would you shut up and do the goddamn reading for once?" The new voice was Tomás. "You're talking about offender profiling. The HCU program is *geographic* profiling."

"Here we go," Karl's cousin murmured to him. "I've been expecting this blowup all semester. That ignorant loudmouth thinks he's the God of Social Justice."

Karl and his cousin listened as Tomás gave a textbook definition of geographic profiling. "Is that one a good student?" he whispered.

"Intelligent. Works hard. You should take him."

He knew what she meant, but a ripple went through Karl's groin anyway. There was no way Tanya could know her words had sparked images of Tomás naked and leaning against the lectern while Karl ground into his gorgeous ass.

"Okay," said Karl, "since this fellow has done an excellent job explaining why I'm here, I'll describe how this helps us fight human trafficking here in Houston." He looked at Tanya. Her expression was tight-lipped. They'd lost her older sister's daughter two years ago, possibly to *El Sistema*. It was the reason this was their life.

He began explaining how analyzing multiple locations of disappearances could eliminate suspects by reason of opportunity. As Alan began yelling about governmental spying, Tomás said, "It's called Google Earth." *Tomás is damn smart. He would make an excellent cop*, Karl thought. Then the idea hit him. *He would be perfect for this operation.*

Or he *would* be after three years' experience, but this judge's son needed someone by 5:00 p.m. Shit. These were extreme circumstances, but how likely was it the department would accept assistance from someone with zero training?

The boy made a beeline for the door the second Tanya dismissed class, and Karl barely waved good-bye to his cousin so he could catch up.

"Tomás! Wait!"

Tomás shot Karl a withering look, but he didn't slow his pace. "Do I know you?"

Karl had reached Tomás so now he could speak in a low voice. "Oh, yeah, you know me. I would have thought you'd have many fond memories."

"You told me you were a manager at Arby's."

Karl shrugged. "Okay, you caught me. But you told me you were a delivery boy for Pizza Rico."

"I am."

"And a stripper and the star employee of Just Jocks Cleaning Service."

"I can't afford rent plus tuition with one job."

"You didn't say you were a college student."

"You didn't ask."

"Well, my friend, you sure are full of surpr—hey, stop! Why are you so angry?"

Tomás halted at the bus shelter next to the building's side exit. He frowned with exasperation. "I've figured you tops out. I'm 'Triple Tap Tomás.' A guy fucks my ass once, comes back for seconds because it was fun, then fucks me a third time to prove he can have it anytime he wants. I'm an easy bottom. That's what I get. But I guess I'm not the only one who didn't know the code. See, a top never returns for a fourth time until months later because that's his way of telling me I'm just for fucking."

Oh. Karl owed Tomás an apology. "And I did come over a fourth and, uh, fifth time pretty quick, so you thought it meant more. I can explain. First, I'm sorry I hurt you, but—"

Tomás looked away. "'I'm sorry' is good enough, dude. If I understand the rules, I should say no after giving it up the second time, right? But I'm too horny, too dumb or too nice to play games for the sake of figuring out who's interested in me. Not just my ass."

Karl discerned some "protesting too much" beneath legitimate disappointment. Tomás wanted to be used, but perhaps he'd felt the same connection Karl had felt and hadn't let it show. "Tomás, I really *was* interested, but...when you told me online what you did, I didn't think you'd meet me if I told you I'm a cop." Tomás looked down and chewed his lip. "Stripping isn't the cleanest gig, but once I learned it was nude housecleaning, too, it...wouldn't work."

Tomás shrugged. "Yeah, your police world sucks. I wasn't thinking of background checks when I decided on criminal justice. My jobs are worse than no job. If your work requires you to be naked and you want a career change, the only jobs you can get require you to be naked. Even so, I didn't think a decent guy would be ashamed to be with me."

Karl raised his hands to object. "It's seriously my job. Not about shame." He put his hands on Tomás's shoulders. "If you're interested, I want to talk more about us, but first, it seems you're interested in law enforcement, and there's an outside chance the department might need you, like, immediately. We should talk someplace quiet."

"This doesn't look like a coffee shop," Karl said as he pulled into the parking lot of a small, weathered apartment complex. He had a vague recollection there'd been serious incidents at this location.

"You said you wanted to talk someplace private," Tomás said. "I live here."

I said "quiet," not "private." "Okay, but I don't have much time." Karl almost added, "And I need to spend it talking, not stuffing you full of dick," but watching Tomás rub the tattoo on his neck stopped his tongue.

Karl's heart rate quickened as he watched Tomás's ass while the boy walked up one flight of stairs and unlocked a dented door. The tidy studio apartment smelled clean. "Do you work on your own apartment in a jockstrap?"

"Practice makes perfect."

"Anywhere to sit?"

"Just the mattress."

Of course. "I'll stand. Buddy, you mentioned the background check obstacle. What if there was a way around that?"

"How?" Tomás asked.

"I won't lie. The help needed is not something small and would never be asked for under other circumstances."

Tomás handed Karl a glass of ice water. "What do you mean?"

"Something big triggered a need to hit a trafficking ring. Do you know what I'm talking about?"

Tomás shuddered. "*El Sistema?* Those guys give me the creeps."

That wasn't the response Karl had expected. "You actually know members of a trafficking ring?"

"Know of one or two, but not actually know them. There's a guy who comes into KJ's. He has the tattoo."

What tattoo? The vice cops told him nothing. "KJ's? The bar where you strip?"

"Where I dance, you mean."

"Can you describe the tattoo?"

"A black capital letter *E* with a green and brown viper curled around it. Like it's a letter *S*. It's on his chest, but high enough you can see it when his shirt's open."

"Do you know his name? Where he can be found?"

"Not his real name. The guys call him Tiburón, which means shark. I think he used to wear a shark-tooth necklace."

"Jeez, Tomás, you seriously are full of surprises." Karl texted Corley's office. If they already had this information, he'd be pissed.

"I was ninety-nine percent sure when you said 'talk someplace private,' you didn't mean talk."

Karl looked up, his dick stiffening again. "Oh, you have no idea. But the city needs help with *El Sistema* now. The fact you already know someone makes this...tougher."

"What? Why tougher?"

"I wanted to ask for your help, but the more I think the department will go for it, the worse I feel. Even your...awful stoplight tattoo would help."

"How?"

"Police can't have visible tattoos, so no one would suspect you're undercover. I was thinking you'd wear a wire and gather info, but you already have a connection. That makes this a rare opportunity, and I'd bet they'd want to uh…"

"Use me as bait?"

"It's too risky. You're not trained."

"So if it's too risky, you must be here for something else."

"Don't get me revved up." Karl received a text back. Yes, they'd heard rumors about a snake tattoo, but had not confirmed them. Karl should call them with a description of Tiburón.

"You're here for my ass."

Karl swallowed. Yep. Bottom boys and their vanity. Might as well appeal to it. "Okay, it is about your ass."

"Aha."

"But it's about the city needing that ass to get itself inside *El Sistema*." As Karl pieced together that the city had more information than they'd given him, he wondered if the reason they'd considered his plan was his personal ability to find someone like Tomás. Someone expendable. Karl shook his head. "I have to come up with another idea in the next three hours. I need you to describe Tiburón. Then I should split."

"So you're going to take off without fucking me because you don't feel like admitting you want to own my hole, fuck it like a madman, then puff up your chest and walk out, never even thinking about me. Then maybe someday you'll need my ass again and—hey!"

In one motion, Karl leapt on the mattress and roughly shoved Tomás's legs skyward. With his right hand, he gripped the crotch of Tomás's cotton shorts and pulled. Without a second's resistance, they ripped off, and there was Tomás's smooth, perfect hole. The shock of the assault had Tomás scrambling away for a moment, but now he remained still, his breathing hard, his dick erect and his eyes wild with need.

Karl growled as he fingered Tomás and whispered in his ear. "Why did you get that stoplight tattoo?"

"What? A friend told me to get it. That it would be good for me. I like it."

"A friend? Stud pup, a light that's always green stops no one. They just keep coming. Everyone gets that ass, and everyone knows it. Is that what your friend wanted to tell the world? Who is he?"

"He doesn't matter."

"Does everyone get this ass?"

"No. But I've never stopped you. You've fucked me every time I've seen you."

Lust shot through Karl, and he rolled on top of Tomás. "We're keeping the streak going."

Tomás always had expensive micro-thin condoms with him. The delay while Tomás struggled with the wrapper made Karl tense with impatience. He lubed Tomás with feral urgency. But less than thirty seconds after he'd slipped on the condom, he was in heaven, sinking into Tomás's warm, velvety smooth hole. Tomás whimpered and gasped, which made Karl smile. Tomás may not have been a prostitute, but the green light said it all. Just about everyone *did* get his ass, but Tomás still couldn't help but moan with Karl's every stroke. The fact that someone who received so much fucking squirmed and struggled under Karl's dick, and that his hole felt so perfect and tight, filled Karl with pride and hunger. He began to slam in and out of Tomás's mounds, rolling the younger man's thighs farther back so he could watch his own cock conquering that magnificent bubble ass, stabbing again and again. The sensation of warm pleasure surrounding his dick rose to his gut and then to his temples. Tomás's beautiful mouth, contorted with passion, his muscular body, and his warm, welcoming hole, soon had Karl light-headed with frenzy. He had no idea how long he'd been mercilessly pumping into Tomás, but when the younger man cried out, *"Eres bien verga,"* and bit down on a pillow to muffle his moans, Karl went out of his mind with ecstasy. The surge of his orgasm ripped through him, and he came deep inside Tomás with a series of growls. At the same time, Tomás's head began to thrash back and forth, his teeth still gripping the pillow. He convulsed as he shot into his own hand.

"You said in Spanish that I'm 'good dick' didn't you?" asked Karl. "That's nice to know because I'd forgotten how much I missed this."

Tomás tapped his fingers against his ass, still hosting Karl's cock. "Missed this or missed me?"

Karl smiled and kissed Tomás on the forehead. "Both."

As Tomás cleaned off, Karl took a minute to check his texts and discovered bad news. The necessary tracking device wasn't available. His plan was shot. He closed his eyes in frustration. At least Tomás wouldn't be put in danger.

"Buddy, I promise I'll help you with a career with the force, but I can't ask for assistance on this."

"But my stoplight tattoo. I thought I'd be perfect." Tomás grabbed Karl's arm. "If I'm your best bet, I want in." Tomás looked Karl in the eye. "In fact, why don't you tell your bosses I'll volunteer only if, when they're reviewing my application, they remember my tarnished background actually helped them with this case?"

Karl inhaled. Tomás had a point. Besides, were there other options? *For the judge's boy. For my cousin. But please God don't let this boy get hurt.*

"Okay." Karl nodded toward the window. A tall man was heading toward his car. He'd been hoping someone would pass by to test the accuracy of Tomás's descriptions before he got details on Tiburón.

"Have you seen that guy before?"

Tomás went to the window, not caring he was still nude. "No, don't think so."

Karl chuckled. "Stop flashing the neighbors. Give me a description of that man."

Tomás raised his eyebrows. "He's all right looking. He's got the height and build for a good top, but he's got nothing on you."

Karl snorted. "That's not what I—"

"—About six-two. Big, wavy George Lucas hair, but light brown. Beige suit, white button-down shirt, solid dark tie— navy or black. Brown leather belt."

"Uh, all right. Anything else?"

"Shoes had a heel so he's probably closer to six or six-one. No rings on his left hand. His black leather briefcase blocked my view of the right. No visible tattoos or scars. He got into a white Mazda Miata."

"Christ, what was the plate number?"

"No idea, but it was New Mexico, not Texas, and had a BUSH/CHENEY '04 sticker which tells you it's not a new vehicle."

"Guess those criminal justice classes worked." He handed Tomás his notepad. "Write down a description of Tiburón for me." It seemed more and more like Tomás would be the key to this op working.

Karl picked up his phone. "Get dressed. We need to get your ear pierced right now." He ignored Tomás's confused look as he left a message on Lieutenant Corley's voice mail. "Lieutenant, I got the message we don't have the device. El Paso PD has the test prototype. It needs to be on the next flight to Hobby." He didn't usually act this demanding with his superiors, but they had to know how much of this shit-dangerous situation was made worse by them not listening to him time and again. Still, he softened his voice as he added, "Text me when I should head to the airport to pick it up. Thanks."

* * *

Academy training should last six months, but Karl had been foolish to hope the department would at least give Tomás a crash course in self-defense. The two-hour prep session focused only on mistakes that would endanger their case and safety protocols to ensure that no "real" officer would be at risk. They showed him a photo of Jared, the judge's son, but didn't give the kid's name or explain who he was. They wasted time emphasizing that the "earring" they were putting on Tomás cost a fortune.

No one bothered to wish him luck or warn him to be careful. He almost expected to hear, "Let the bad guys ream your ass until we feel like rescuing you." HPD did *not* have someone else inside the ring, so what options would Tomás have? Karl's stomach hurt with frustration.

Hours later, Karl sat hunched in the back of an unmarked car watching Tomás stand in front of the stripper bar. "When did they start making business suits specifically for slut boys?" Karl had wondered aloud in front of Tomás. When Tomás said he'd made the suit, Karl had said, "Once again, you're full of surprises."

Tomás wore a tight-fitting black blazer, under which his tan, sculpture-perfect torso was bare except for a half-undone skinny tie. Tomás periodically took off the jacket, and Karl could see the formfitting pants not only hugged his hips without a belt, but were tailored to reveal the top third of Tomás's ass. He had a prop—a cheap overnight bag stuffed with clothes. He kept bending over, pretending to look in his bag, but he was actually just showing off his incredible rump. *Did he really need to do that? Or was it for Karl?* Even only hours after screwing him, the sight of those bare mounds had Karl imagining bending Tomás over and violating every public decency ordinance.

* * *

Tomás's ear hurt. He had to dig his fingernails into his palm
to keep from fiddling with the device. He stood outside KJ's,
listening to the thumping music that accompanied each go-go
boy. He was glad for the breeze that tempered the insuffer-
able Houston heat. Finally, after nearly two hours, there was
Tiburón, who looked him up and down.

"*Cuánto para el culo, putito?*" Tiburón said, stopping to
grope and squeeze Tomás's buttcheeks. He pressed the bulge of
his pants into Tomás. "How much for, say...three hours?"

Tomás looked away. "I'm not sure. I don't normally do
this." Even with the police watching, standing next to Tiburón
unnerved him. The other dancers had been wary long before
anyone knew he was connected to *El Sistema*. Tiburón was too
young and handsome to need street hustlers. Tonight he was
dressed a bit like Tomás. A blazer and dress pants, a white shirt
with enough buttons open to reveal part of the *Sistema* tattoo.

"Sooner or later," Tiburón said, nodding toward the bar,
"everyone strutting on the stage in there winds up standing out
here. So what happened?"

"The last person looking out for me in this town is gone."
Tomás said, looking down at his bag. "So no friends. One too
many enemies. As soon as I get cash, *me voy.*"

Tiburón nodded slowly. "I can help." He ran his index finger
down Tomás's torso and then rubbed the boy's stomach in small
circles. Tomás's gut tightened in both heat and fear. "Let me get
a quick drink, say hello to some people and hit the ATM inside.
Un minuto, chulo."

Thirty minutes later, a rusty gray van pulled up. Two men
got out and grabbed Tomás. He barely struggled.

* * *

The Vice Unit vehicle slowly slid onto the road. Karl told himself he didn't mind. They weren't trying to stop the van. In fact, they weren't even the lead since two FBI task forces had been put on alert. What he *did* mind was deliberately letting the van reach its destination. Yes, that GPS earring made sure they tracked the van all the way down the Southwest Freeway to an area rife with crime, and of course, they had units in the area. But over the radio, Karl and the vice cops in the front seat heard they'd hit a snag. No one had anticipated a fortified bunker. As they sped down the freeway, all Karl could think about was what *El Sistema's* men might have done to Tomás in the van and what they might be doing to him now.

Tomás had anticipated the chloroform before it hit his face, but even holding his breath and acting like it had gotten to him faster didn't spare him. At least he woke up sooner than he would have otherwise. He was naked on a cool cement floor, his vision blurry and his head buzzing. His rectum throbbed with hot pain. He sat up, noticing he wasn't cuffed or guarded. He tried to focus on his surroundings. Doors on two walls, no windows, a couple of wooden chairs and some metal boxes. There was also a shiny black disc on one wall that was likely a camera. He needed to lie back down and pretend he was still out until his head cleared.

Less than five minutes later, there was that asshole, Tiburón.

"You're awake, *putito*. Good."

Tomás used the wall behind him to help him stand up. "What the hell is your problem?"

Tiburón mimed a confused shrug. "*No hay bronca*. I want to fuck you, that's all. But this time while you're awake so I can hear you moan." He began to undo his belt. "Just once more before you reach Matamoros."

"Matamoros?"

"You needed to leave town, right? I've done you a favor."

Tomás felt his earlobe. The tracking device was still there. He closed his eyes and imagined simply lifting his legs and allowing this man to invade him. Tomás believed the expression "nice guys finish last" was, in his case, "nice guys always get fucked." Tiburón stroked his thick dick.

"So now you owe me. Fighting would be a mistake."

Tomás nodded but didn't want to get fucked. *Again.* The longer he played along, the more time to get rescued. "*Bueno, papi.* But I want to be yours, okay? Don't let me be a slave in Matamoros or wherever. Keep me yourself. I will be good to you."

Tiburón's eyes narrowed. "What?"

Tomás got on his knees and started jerking the man's dick. "Just keep me in your apartment. I can sleep in a corner. I'll clean every day. You can fuck me constantly. I wouldn't stop you. I couldn't." Tomás didn't like that he was getting hard at his own words, but he'd worry about his screwed-up head later. "And...if you want, you can give my ass to your friends. Or sell it if you need money." This is where he had to make the offer look real by pulling back. He shot Tiburón a beseeching look. "But, please, your friends have to use condoms. The only one I want bare is you, *papi.*"

Tiburón let out a low growl, rumbling with lust. He ran his hands through Tomás's hair and then shoved him onto his back.

"*Ahorita, ofrécemelo.*" Offer it to me, now.

"Yes, yes, *papi,*" Tomás whimpered as he lifted his legs. "*Espera, papi. Momentito.*" He spit into his own hand and lubed himself as well as possible. Why was his heart racing with need? He shouldn't want his ass pumped by a man who would sell him, but he thought of a reason why it was okay this once. How often does the City of Houston need someone to lose his ass to rescue innocent victims? *Go ahead. Give it up. Slut and hero at the same time.*

Ay, *goddamn*. Not enough lube. Not ready. "Stop! Not yet! I'll give it to you, but...ay!" Tiburón was not stopping, and the burn was too great. Tomás bit his own hand to stop screaming, but that made Tiburón ram harder.

I might be easy, but you will not fucking hurt me.

Tomás took his right hand and clawed deeply at Tiburón's face, at the same time leaning forward to bite down on Tiburón's forearm. Tiburón's scream was cut off by a gasp, the wind going out of him as Tomás kneed him in the gut and toppled him onto his side. Tomás landed on top of Tiburón, putting one leg on Tiburón's chest but grabbing his dick at the same time. He stroked gently, not knowing how long rescue would be. "Look, I'm serious about you owning my ass, *papi*. But I need you to go slower. If you injure me I can't be as good to you as I want, can I? So please?"

Tiburón looked more angry than frightened. "*Pinche putito*, I'm going to fuck you as hard as I want, but now there will be others in the room. If you try that again, we'll break your arm."

Tomás didn't move. "Okay, I'll be good, but you can trust me, *papi*, only if I can trust you."

Both doors burst open. Operatives in black bulletproof vests rushed in. Tomás immediately stood up and put his hands in the air.

The first man to reach him removed his earring. "Device recovered," he said into a headset as other hands patted Tomás on the back and ushered him out of the room before he could see what happened to Tiburón.

Outside he was swathed in a blanket and handed a cup of water. Through flashing lights, he watched the chaos of arrests and shouted orders. Moments later, Karl was giving him a brief hug.

"Hey, brave man, this went better than we could have imagined. We got the judge's son back. Half a dozen young women, too. They were in another part of the bunker. And now we know there's another site a hundred miles south of here." He squeezed Tomás's shoulder. "You okay? Did they hurt you?"

Tomás knew he'd be given a rape kit shortly, and Karl was sure to find out about it then. But he blinked and looked Karl in the eye. "I'm sure I'm doing better than the other guy."

Karl jogged up the stairs, having brought Tomás's prescription painkillers as promised, but he'd also brought flowers and some dinner. Tomás opened the door in his jockstrap. Karl inhaled at the sight, making a sizzling sound through his teeth. Dinner could wait. Karl headed for the fridge. "So, my man, this is the biggest break they've gotten against traffickers in years. The chief of police is rewarding me with a move up to Vice and a bonus. I'm taking a week's vacation on a private beach in Martinique. If you come with me, I could have you nude nonstop for seven days."

Tomás gave Karl a simmering look. He'd told Karl to be sure to put sex in every conversation, saying he didn't want things to be any different after the attack. "That sounds incredible, but could I be nude nonstop on your mattress instead of the beach? You know, no sunburn in sensitive areas?"

Karl grinned. "To pay for all that incredible sex you'll get, will you learn some French? Maybe take a course a couple hours a day?" Karl didn't mention learning French had no connection to Martinique. The federal judge had been impressed with Tomás and told them he'd get that interview. But Karl hoped they'd eventually work together in Vice, and traffickers were moving women and children in from Haiti. They needed an agent who could listen in on conversations held in a rapid-fire combination of Spanish and French. They hadn't found anyone.

"Je parle Français...mais...tu as besoin de quelqu'un qui comprend Créole, oui?"

"Uh...what?"

"I was trying to say I know French fairly well, and I was gonna ask if we could spend those couple hours a day doing... something else." Tomás let out a small laugh. "But I realized you probably were thinking of the department's need for someone who understands Haitian French, not high school French, right?" Tomás stretched and looked away, as if absentmindedly spreading his thighs wasn't a deliberate enticement.

Karl raised his eyebrows, once again amazed at his young friend, but he couldn't resist the invitation. He slid his fingers between Tomás's legs. "Yeah, you guessed my game. But we do need something else to do for two hours a day. At least." He pressed insistently on Tomás's hot, tight hole.

"This is when you usually say I'm always full of surprises."

"You are. And you will be in more ways than one after I change my name to Karl 'Surprises' Wilkes." He grinned, seeing his wickedness had shocked Tomás. "And I hope you keep surprising me for a very long time." He kissed Tomás's mouth deeply. "A very, very long time. Our adventure hasn't even begun."

BULLETPROOF

Logan Zachary

Stop, or I'll shoot."

The suspect turned and fired.

BANG!

The bullet hit him in the center of his chest and knocked him on his perfect ass. Officer Marc Toledo lay where he fell, gasping for breath. His lungs refused to allow him any air. He inhaled with all of his force and tried to suck in as much oxygen as he could get, before he passed out.

A shadow passed across the sun and stood above him with the sawed-off shotgun. Had he reloaded already? Did he have another...?

His arm came up with his Glock and aimed without thought, pure reflex. A click pierced his ears as he pulled the trigger, and the world turned red. Warm, crimson rain drenched him. At least, he wished it were rain, and not the perp's brains and blood.

That was until the dead body landed on top of him. The shotgun discharged as it hit the ground.

His ears rang, and the world felt as if he had a glass fishbowl on his head.

"Breathe," his partner yelled at him. "Breathe."

The pressure on his chest released, and he gasped, his lungs and diaphragm finally working again, as oxygen rushed in.

"Fuck." Toledo knew this one was going to bruise, both ends. He rolled into a bloody pool on the ground as he tried to get out from under the dead body. He spat the shit out of his mouth and pushed slowly onto his hands and knees.

His partner, Officer Sam Reynolds, pulled on a pair of rubber gloves before he extended his hand and helped him to his unsteady feet.

Why is there cauliflower on the ground? flashed through his mind, and then he was glad he hadn't asked that out loud. His ears were still ringing, and he had an intense pressure deep inside each canal. His partner's voice sounded so far-off, despite being less than a foot away.

He opened his mouth. His hand went to the place the bullet went into. He felt a single hole in his uniform and a piece of metal in the crease of the Kevlar vest.

"Didn't he have a shotgun?"

"Yes, sir," came a muffled response from his partner.

"Then..." Toledo's finger dug into the one hole. "Why..."

"Um, all right, fuck, shit, damn. I shot you," Officer Reynolds admitted.

"Why?"

"The perp moved."

Toledo closed his eyes and shook his cotton-filled head. "Then why didn't you shoot him?"

"I tried, but I missed."

Toledo looked at his blood-splattered Glock and then down to his holster. He slipped his wet gun into the dirty leather case. Blood and brain sprayed across the ground.

Fuck, why did he always get stuck with the rookies?

"That was so cool when his..." Officer Reynolds stopped talking.

Officer Toledo rubbed his ass and shook his head. No criminal had ever shot him, but three of his previous partners had, and this rookie was number four.

After filling out all of the paperwork involved in the shooting case, Toledo was off duty for a few days while his superiors reviewed the incident. The incident having been videotaped by *Channel 5 News* would help show it was all in self-defense, and that he had saved two small kids and their mother.

He doubted it would play out as well for his rookie. He picked up the paperwork and reread what he had written. He added, *After giving my partner the signal to shoot me to distract the perp from hurting his family, Officer Reynolds discharged his firearm. The bullet knocked me to the ground. The gunman stood over me, out of the line of fire from his family, which made it safer to subdue him—until he leveled the shotgun at my head. Lethal force was employed at that time.*

He stood up and walked into the next room where Officer Reynolds filled out his report. "Put in your report, that I gave you the signal to shoot me to draw the perp away from his family and get them out of the line of fire." He flipped to the page and showed the rookie what he had just written.

"Why?" was all the young man asked.

"Everyone makes mistakes, live and learn by them." He flipped left to turn it in.

After dropping off his papers, Toledo headed to the locker room to change and get ready for his doctor's visit. As he removed his bloody shirt and vest, he pulled out a plastic garbage bag.

He noticed an ugly purple and blue circle was already forming underneath his hairy skin. He touched it and cringed. "Fuck, that hurts."

John Beckman, his first rookie, approached with a white bottle. "Take four now, and two every four hours for the next two days," his buddy tossed him the Advil.

"Thanks." Toledo opened the bottle and poured five round orange pills into his hand. He swallowed all five. One more wouldn't hurt. He sat down on the wooden bench on his bruised bottom and groaned. He kicked his shoes off in his locker. He picked up the plastic garbage bag and tossed his bloody, sweaty socks into it.

Did he want to shower here or at home? He sat there with his head in his hands.

A hand touched the center of his back. "You okay?" Officer Reynolds asked.

The warm hand felt great on his sore back. Reynolds was such a young kid. Had he ever been that young? That green? That inexperienced? Toledo shook his head. "Just trying to get motivated to hit the shower and go home."

Reynolds opened the locker next to him and sat his empty holster inside. "They took my gun and my badge."

Toledo said nothing as he undid his belt and pants.

"Thanks for covering for me." He touched Toledo's bare shoulder.

Something passed from the kid and into him, giving him the energy to finish what he started. He was the role model here, he couldn't disappoint. Pulling the zipper down, he slipped his pants down to his ankles and carefully sat back down. His boxers bunched into his sweaty crack.

Officer Reynolds watched his protector in great awe. He knew he should be fired, and he still possibly could be, but for

the lie Toledo put in his report. He might have dodged that
bullet. His body shivered. Would he dodge the next one?

"Don't go second-guessing yourself," Toledo's voice startled
him out of his thoughts. "The kids are safe, you did well." The
pain throbbed in his body, but he wouldn't let Reynolds know
that. He threw his pants into the bag, grabbed his towel and
headed to the shower. He could feel Reynolds's eyes on his ass.
Was he looking for the bruise or...? He didn't wait to find out.

He stopped at the urinal before hitting the shower. As he
turned the water on, he stepped out of his boxers and tossed
them over the water knob. The hot spray stung his body, but it
felt great relaxing the muscles in his back and legs. He turned to
face the shower, and the force of the water hurt his bruises.

The soap containers were full of the amber liquid, and he
pressed the pump to get some out. He soaped his head and hair
first, washing the blood and brain material down the drain. Red
rivulets streaked across the hexagonal white tiles.

He'd probably have to have another HIV test due to the
blood exposure. The perp's blood would also be tested.

He closed his eyes and inhaled the steam, pulling it deep
into his lungs; it hurt as he expanded his chest, but he knew it
would make him feel better sooner. One of the officers had had
a collapsed lung after being shot, and several broken ribs, but at
least their vests had saved their lives.

The shower next to him started up.

Toledo turned his back to the spray and let the water pound
his shoulders and upper back. Out of the corner of his eye, he
looked at Reynolds, and his heart almost stopped.

Underneath his rookie uniform, that lean, skinny body was
chiseled and buff. Muscles rippled beneath a tan body. His male
pattern of body hair made him look like a model for a Titan
Video cover. He had a bodacious ass. As he turned around, he

was definitely a show-er, and Toledo wondered how much of a grower.

Water cascaded over Reynolds's beautiful body and washed all Toledo's pain down the drain. He could feel his own body start to react to the visual stimulation; slowly his thick penis was getting bigger, longer. He reached for the soap and washed his growing arousal, which only made matters worse. He turned and switched the water from scalding to cold, sending shivers over his body, and hopefully deflating his excitement.

Reynolds washed his body, seemingly unaware of the effect he was having on his senior officer. "How do you feel?"

"What?" Toledo was taken aback by his question, until he realized he meant pain, not pleasure. "Still a bit sore, but the Advil is kicking in, and the shower is kind of helping." *If you only knew,* he thought.

"I can drive you to the clinic if you need a ride," Reynolds offered. Water sprayed off his body and landed on Toledo's, burning him where it touched.

Toledo rinsed off one more time and turned off the water. He grabbed his boxers and splashed through the water on the tile floor to retrieve his towel. He dried his face and ran the towel over his head once, before wrapping it around his narrow hips. His bare feet left footprints across the floor leading back to his locker.

The shower had refreshed him, but Reynolds's naked body had excited him. He pulled out a clean pair of white boxers and quickly pulled them on over his damp body. He briskly wiped his hairy chest and legs before standing on his towel.

Reynolds came back to the lockers. "I really have nothing to do; I can drive you to the clinic."

"Sure," Toledo agreed.

"Cool, let me get dressed, and I'll be ready." He dropped

his towel and bent over to reach into his locker. His beautiful buttcheeks spread and a pink hole winked at the older cop. His ass was so perfect.

He licked his lips and thought, *Why doesn't this job ever get any easier?* And his boxers became tighter.

"The doctor gave me a clean bill of health," Toledo said, as he reentered the waiting room.

Reynolds stood as he approached. "I'm glad to hear it. Are you ready to go home?"

"I just need to pick up my prescription, and then I'll be set."

"Maybe we can stop and get something to eat too." Reynolds's expression would have worked alone if Toledo's stomach hadn't growled at the time.

"Sounds like a plan."

They rode in silence to the pharmacy, and Toledo ran in.

Reynolds tapped on the steering wheel as he waited. He noticed a Mexican restaurant next door and ran in to order food. He was back at the car just as Toledo left the pharmacy.

"It smells great in here," he said as he clicked his seat belt.

"I picked up supper for us." Reynolds's hand squeezed Toledo's knee.

"Perfect," he said, his leg burning from the other man's touch. His arousal returned in full force.

They ate everything. Not a chip or a drop of salsa was left.

Reynolds stood to leave. "Well, I should be heading home now."

Toledo stood, but his head swirled and his body started to sway.

Reynolds rushed to his side and grabbed his arm. "Are you okay?" He searched his partner's eyes and noticed how they fluttered and weren't able to focus on him. His hand caressed his hairy forearm as he spoke, trying to bring him back to his body, back to his senses. "That's okay, just breathe, nice and slow. Take a deep breath and hold it."

The room stopped spinning, and the waves of nausea disappeared. Toledo took a deep breath and his eyes zoomed in on Reynolds's lips. Full and fleshy, pink and moist, he wondered how they would taste and how good of a kisser his partner was. Wow! Where did that come from? Seeing his partner naked had never affected him like this before. His body swayed to the right.

Reynolds wrapped his arms around him and held him close. Their necks rested along each other, coarse whiskers rubbing. The manly scent of their sweat and soap filled the air. "I think I should spend the night, just to make sure you are okay."

Toledo didn't refuse. He wrapped his arms around him and held him tight. His dick grew hard in his pants as it pressed against his leg.

"Where's your bedroom?" Reynolds whispered into his ear.

He let go with one hand and pointed to a hallway.

Reynolds sidestepped and wrapped his arm around his partner's waist to lead him down the hall. He helped him out of his clothes and under the covers.

Reynolds slipped his bare legs into the cool sheets. He stretched his long legs out as Toledo rolled onto his back. He held his breath, waiting for the scolding that never came.

"Do you have enough room?"

"Yeah, sure."

"Could you move a little closer?" Toledo rolled onto his side, turning his back to Reynolds.

Reynolds scooted closer and spooned the other man's body.

His hairy legs wrapped around. His hairy chest pressed against Toledo's back as his arm wrapped over him, pulling him closer. His erection grew to full length with three beats of his heart and nestled between his partner's cheeks as their breathing fell into sync. His fingers combed through the pelt on his chest and rolled over an erect nipple.

A low moan escaped from Toledo.

"Am I hurting you?"

"Oh no, it feels great to be held." He squeezed his buttcheeks together, letting the rookie know he knew.

Reynolds pushed his hips forward and pressed his pelvis into Toledo's fleshy ass. Bruised and tender as the older cop was, the excitement of the hard cock acted as a balm to ease his pain. Reynolds held him in his arms for a long time, while his cock oozed into his underwear. A wet spot grew as they lay there.

Toledo rolled onto his back and looked into Reynolds's eyes.

Reynolds pulled the sheets down and rolled onto his knees. He leaned forward and kissed the black-and-blue spot in the center of Toledo's chest. He kissed around the edge of the spot. His lips brushed over a nipple and drew it into his mouth. His teeth rolled the nub back and forth.

Moans of pleasure rose from Toledo. His hands grabbed Reynolds's head and guided his mouth to his own. Their tongues flicked out and touched: raspy, wet, and hungry. Their tips rolled around each other, as their mouths opened wider and their lips met. Instantly, they kissed, deeply and passionately.

Reynolds crawled over Toledo's body and straddled him. His bulge brushed against the throbbing one beneath him. He ground his hips down and rubbed erection to erection. Damp cotton covered both.

Toledo broke the kiss as he gasped for air.

Reynolds kissed him one more time and started to lick down his neck over to his earlobe. He nibbled on the flap of skin and teased it as his tongue worked its way into his ear.

Toledo thought he was going to shoot his wad.

Reynolds trailed his tongue down the senior cop's razor-stubble-covered cheek and down his neck. His hands stroked down his torso as he licked lower and lower. His finger found the elastic waistband and dug underneath it. His fingers rolled over the hair and lowered the boxers.

Toledo's thick pubic bush burst out of its confines as the fabric went lower and lower. His cock strained against the white cotton, trailing a line of precum across the material. His fat mushroom head burst out of its confines and a huge drop flew across his stomach.

Reynolds licked it up as he moved down Toledo's torso. His chin traced along his cock and down to his furry balls. He wiggled his jaw side to side all the way down his shaft. He inhaled deeply as the musky ball sweat rose from the hot hairy sac below. His lips kissed the wet tip as his tongue licked into the opening.

More clear fluid poured out of the senior cop's balls.

Reynolds had to open his mouth and slowly swallow the thick dick, inch by inch.

Toledo threw his head back and thrust his hips up.

Reynolds grabbed his low hanging balls and controlled his thrusts. He swallowed and sucked, drew down hard on Toledo's sensitive skin and swirled his tongue around and around. A finger released his sac and slipped between his cheeks, which were moist, hot and hairy, exploring the opening.

"Yes, yes, yes," was all Toledo could say.

Reynolds used his other hand to pull down his own underwear. His balls swung free and his dick flipped up and tapped along his own belly. How he wanted to bury it deep inside that tight hole. He licked down the shaft and along the crease between the pelvis and leg, brushing the other man's balls as he went deeper.

Toledo sprang up onto his knees, but Reynolds turned him over. His bruised butt came into view; despite the black-and-blue mark, it was an amazing sight. Reynolds pushed him down on all fours and moved between his legs. He spread those beautiful cheeks and licked along the crease.

Toledo's back extended, and he rose up, only to be bent over again.

Reynolds's tongue passed over the tight hole and felt it twitch. He circled around the muscle and tried to tease it open. He reached around and grabbed the swinging dick and started to stroke it.

More precum oozed out of Toledo and he pushed back onto the rookie's face.

Reynolds's tongue worked in deeper and tasted him: man, sweat and musk. Drool rolled down his balls and dripped onto the bed. His hand worked his dick faster and faster.

Toledo reached for his bedside table and pulled out a condom and lube. He passed it back without a word.

Reynolds felt as if he owed him his ass for saving it today, but...if this is what he wanted, what they wanted...he pulled his tongue out and wiped the back of his hand across his face. Rising up, he ripped the condom packet open and slipped it on.

He poured lube into his hand and smoothed it over his dick and then applied more to Toledo's ass. His finger slipped in and tested the other man's readiness.

Toledo's hips rocked back and forth on his hand, letting him know he was ready. He spread his legs wider and crouched down lower.

Reynolds slid his cock along the crease, pausing on the opening. He pressed on it and pulled back, only to reapply pressure to the tight opening. He felt it give slightly and pushed harder. His fat tip popped in and the rest of the shaft entered easier.

Toledo's moan was low and guttural, coming from deep within a primal place. He pushed back until he felt the cock stop. He bore down on the dick as it slowly retracted. The increased pressure gained a groan of pure pleasure from behind him. He smiled as he relaxed and allowed another thrust inside. Back and forth they rode, slow and deliberate, savoring each inch as it entered or exited.

Reynolds pulled back and popped out of Toledo's tight ass.

Toledo rolled over onto his back after thrusting a pillow under his hips. He spread his legs wide and waited for reentry.

Reynolds moved between his legs and lifted the low hangers out of the way. He inserted himself in to the hilt. He reached forward and grabbed the raging hard-on in front of him. He stroked the lubed hand up and down the shaft as he entered and exited him, matching their motions perfectly.

"Faster," Toledo said. His eyes were closed as he held his legs wide apart for deep penetration.

Reynolds doubled his pace, skin slapping against skin as he jacked the dripping cock harder and harder. Sweat poured over his brow and burned his eyes; he wiped it away quickly and returned to his task, faster, harder, deeper.

He swallowed hard, knowing he was close. He felt the tight ass clamp down on his cock as he dove in and that was all he could take; his balls exploded, filling the condom. The eruption slammed against the prostate and set it off.

Toledo's balls pulled up and shot his load over his torso. Wave after wave of hot thick cum flowed like a volcano. His ass spasmed and set off another orgasm deep inside.

Another wave of cum erupted in the condom and sent another prostate orgasm out of Toledo's cock. Round and round the pleasure flowed between the two men. Reynolds flopped down on the bed next to Toledo, both men spent and gasping for air, Toledo more so due to his bruised ribs. Reynolds pulled the sheet over them and they slowly drifted off to sleep.

The clock radio blared as Jon Bon Jovi sang about getting shot through the heart.

Toledo shot up and hit the OFF button. The pain returned as soon as he sat up. "God, I know that feeling."

Reynolds bounded out of bed and returned with Toledo's pills and a glass of water. "Here you go." His morning wood bounced in front of him.

He took his pills and drank the water before lying back down. He closed his eyes and waited for the pain to subside. Toledo felt a gentle hand on his chest that rubbed him carefully in a small circle. "Thanks."

"It was my fault in the first place that you were hurt; just as the song said, I'm to blame."

"It's all a learning process." He reached up and caught Reynolds's hand and held it to his chest. "And I need to learn that I'm not bulletproof."

Reynolds leaned over and kissed him. "Maybe I can remind you."

Toledo squeezed his hand. "As long as you promise not to shoot me again."

"I promise, but you never know how my aim is going to be."

ROADWORK

Gregory L. Norris

Roadwork detail on Lewis Lane, a barely traveled stretch of single-lane asphalt running parallel to the Route 121 overpass, was an assignment for rookies, thought O'Keefe. A real no-brain job. Then Officer Jack White breezed past him, and O'Keefe caught a hint of the other man's scent. He breathed it in; sweet and heady, at first he assumed the smell originated in the wild tangles of overgrown meadow lining the sides of Lewis Lane. An instant after thinking this, Kevin O'Keefe, a ten-year veteran of the town's police force, realized the scent was all Jack White's, a hint of clean male sweat mixed with testosterone. The smell of his excitement. The smell of sex.

"Hey, man," Whitey said, a trace of nerves infusing his voice. He wore his expensive shades, silver in black frames, so O'Keefe couldn't be sure if the other policeman was avoiding direct eye contact, though he suspected as much, the final nail in a particular coffin.

"Yeah, hey," O'Keefe fired back, along with the offer of his knuckles, which Whitey tapped.

Suddenly, most of it made sense. O'Keefe drew in another breath. Sweat—the rookie cop's—and who knew what else? Who'd conjured that kind of excitement with his new partner on this lame late-August assignment?

A stir of motion teased the corner of O'Keefe's eye. He turned toward the source: the road crew working in no particular hurry to fix the section of damaged pavement. O'Keefe again focused on an arm covered in a sleeve of ink among the suntanned skin, a handsome face flushed with guilt. That dude with the tattoos and buzz cut had at least provided something interesting to watch while passing the time. So, too, had Jack White.

"How bored are you, dude?" Whitey asked, breaking O'Keefe's train of thought.

In any other conversation leading up to this one, O'Keefe would have joked about pulling out his service piece and shooting himself in the head. Gruesome as it sounded, apart from the view, the Lewis Lane detail at the end of a long, hot summer had turned out to be the most tedious schedule coverage in recent years.

O'Keefe leaned his butt against his truck and tucked his thumb into his gun belt, assuming a classic policeman's pose. "Man, you don't know how bored. But I think it's almost over."

Whitey tipped a glance at the road crew. Lewis Lane still bore the scars of the broken water pipe that had taken out about a hundred feet of road, but far less of it. Four days here had left O'Keefe pining for his regular duties spent riding in the cruiser, responding to domestic disturbance calls, rowdy punks hanging out where they weren't wanted and the occasional fender bender.

Now, the shittiest detail in town, which he'd pulled the short straw on, as had the rookie, no longer seemed so dull. In another day, the work would be done, and Whitey's dark, dirty secret would vanish back into the lazy, long summer shadows.

O'Keefe studied the young police officer, his junior by a decade. The blond crew cut beneath that baseball cap was perfect around the edges. Whitey was shorter by several inches. Classic nose. Face neatly shaved. A body so lean and muscular, more than once in the boredom of guarding Lewis Lane from nonexistent motorists, O'Keefe had joked to himself that the dude's uniform looked spray painted onto him. His face was above average in terms of looks, and the longer O'Keefe stared, the more he realized how attractive the rookie was.

Officer White...well, he was fucking someone on the road crew, O'Keefe was convinced. That bit of intelligence caused his cock to toughen, to grow sweaty and awkward trapped in his uniform pants and a pair of briefs that felt suddenly, brutally tight.

"So," Whitey sighed. "Another full day of this shit almost behind us, eh?"

O'Keefe tried to ignore his aching erection. Even his baseball cap, bearing the town's police emblem, tried to squeeze him. Whitey smelled hot, good. *Primal*, of rough and masculine sex; sex among the sedge. And now it became clear exactly where the deed was being perpetrated. He'd seen the evidence, and you didn't need to be Sherlock Holmes or Mike Hammer to solve this particular case.

Whitey leaned against the door to O'Keefe's truck, fumbled with his wedding ring, and avoided direct eye contact behind his silver shades.

"Hold the fort, man," O'Keefe said. "I need to take a leak."

Whitey grunted an affirmative, and O'Keefe headed down into the shadow of the nearby 121 overpass, conscious of every step thanks to the swell of his dick. Eventually, he reached the spot where a portable toilet rose up from the meadow flowers and August-roasted grass. The chirrup of insects carried on the afternoon air, uninterrupted and hypnotic. He thought about going into the chemical head and rubbing one out, a fitting end to the day. Instead, he marched around to the back of the blue plastic outhouse, his boots not the first to trample the Timothy and wild chicory flowers behind it.

O'Keefe was a cop and, as such, had a keen eye. He'd noticed the footprints on the first day, and they'd grown steadily more obvious as the week plodded onward. A quick scan with his hawk's gaze found it, right where he expected. A fresh condom had joined the litter of dead soldiers, this newest's tip filled to capacity with whitewash. Discarded in haste, the evidence sealed the investigation.

O'Keefe's cock itched, and his balls were warm and full. The sperm baking in that rubber was Jack White's, he was sure. O'Keefe reached down and squeezed the lump at the front of his uniform pants, then regretted it. Wetness glistened, painting him as guilty as the rookie policeman.

"Oh, fuck it," he grumbled.

Unzipping his pants, O'Keefe carefully removed his cock, wincing at the effort. His piece hung openly in the hot afternoon sunlight, thickest at the middle, a meaty man's dick wreathed in lush curls. Reaching lower, O'Keefe freed his balls and let them hang in the humidity. He caught a whiff of his own sweat, the musk of a set of low-hanging nuts forced to marinate in his underwear all day. They itched. O'Keefe scratched them with one hand while he rubbed out his load with the other.

Eyes half-closed, he envisioned Whitey taking one or more of the construction dudes up here, rolling on a skin, and fucking them, doggy-style in the daisies, especially that tough fucker with the sleeve of tattoos. He'd never guessed such a thing feasible, not with Jack White, recently married in the previous spring. Then again, his inner critic reminded him, it wasn't as if anyone would have expected such a thing of him. Kevin O'Keefe, standing tall in his police uniform, was a snapshot straight out of a policeman's calendar.

Mister August thought about Whitey, sticking it to the big attractive dude with the inked guns and buzz cut, and the first warning of his approaching nut tickled O'Keefe's balls. He fired a shot into the grass, then four more steady blasts, knowing that tomorrow, the last day on this detail, would be above and beyond interesting.

The morning broke warm and muggy, mirroring the previous days on Lewis Lane. A low breeze carried over the construction site, mixing the sweet smell of hay from the meadows with the raw smell of earth. The last length of pipe would be replaced, then the road crew would pack it in, spread tar, and by five o'clock it would all be done.

O'Keefe arrived ten minutes early. Whitey showed twenty late. The rookie smelled of soap, the simple and manly brand with the Irish name, and brought along two iced coffees, one for O'Keefe. Payoff? O'Keefe accepted the bribe and thanked him. And then they waited, keeping watch over a length of road few traveled.

Every day had been the same, at least on the surface. The lazy summer progressed toward its conclusion, disturbed only by the sound of traffic from the overpass and the jackhammering, sawing and other noise from the road crew.

O'Keefe sipped, but his iced coffee did little to quench the dryness in his throat. White's truck sat parked to the side, a deterrent for any driver thinking about taking the shoulder. Drivers? The only two reckless enough to visit Lewis Lane on this morning were a pair of policemen.

Unlike the other days, which O'Keefe had passed by playing Solitaire on his cell phone or ogling White and Tattooed Dude in silence, he stood grim faced and restless, his cock as itchy as his balls, the day too hot, his uniform too tight. He'd jerked off twice the night before and once more in the shower that morning, and still his dick refused to go down.

After each ejaculation, he'd questioned if he'd go through with it. And then O'Keefe's tool re-stiffened, and it became an obsession. Whitey, fucking one of those sweaty construction jocks. It was absolutely conceivable that the secret arrangement had started at some other road job site, the perfect place for a rookie cop to learn the ropes, establish a regular thing with another horn-dog not getting enough on the home front. Some mutually beneficial fuckbuddy sitch that had kept both men sane and satisfied.

Jealousy, green and ugly, gripped him by the sac. O'Keefe shifted uncomfortably, feeling the sweat cling to the center of his shoulder blades, trapped by his uniform shirt, and a glop of heavy perspiration, right under his balls. It was strong emotion, and he didn't much care for it. Mercifully, the jolt evaporated soon after flaring.

"Keep an eye on the fort, would you?" Whitey said, breaking the spell of thoughts O'Keefe had fallen victim to.

"Huh?"

"I need to take a piss. Too much coffee."

O'Keefe offered a wordless tip of the chin to the affirmative and watched Whitey strut off, in the direction of the portable john. Without warning, the day's temperature doubled, and he struggled to breathe despite the ever-present country breeze. In that longer, deeper look, Whitey's ass, high and square and solid, worsened his discomfort. The rookie moved proudly, and O'Keefe imagined the size of the balls swinging below the young policeman's dick.

That dick, O'Keefe imagined, was now stiff.

A second or so later, Whitey confirmed it by adjusting himself. Then he vanished into the overgrowth behind the portable head.

"Oh, fuck," O'Keefe groaned, and started after him.

The walk took less than a minute, but the time stretched out to something far longer in O'Keefe's head. On the final leg, he nearly tripped over his own two feet, gigantic size-thirteens that never faltered in a foot race, whether in pursuit of a suspected criminal or in a policeman's charity run. Steeling himself, O'Keefe ambled the rest of the way down, doing his best to stay quiet.

He tipped a glance toward the road crew. It was break time, apparently. Two of the guys that he could see were stretched out across the grass, grabbing sun or some Zs. Another stood off to one side of the open gouge in the road, talking on his cell phone and sipping water from a plastic bottle. O'Keefe tried to identify Whitey's good buddy through a process of elimination, only sweat dripped into his eyes, and its sting stopped that part of the investigation.

O'Keefe wiped his brow to see he'd reached the last road-block to his destination: the blue obelisk. Like the hike down from Lewis Lane, rounding it passed in heavy seconds. He tromped over the flattened grass to the back of the porta-john, not quite sure what he was seeing at first, only impressed by the genius of it. Had he not found the condoms, not tracked the trail of flattened grass, not smelled the sex on the other cop's hot flesh, O'Keefe never would have guessed anything was going on during Whitey's long visits to head. Nobody would. The overpass loomed beside them, too close for anyone traveling up there to see down. If you were a man in the can, you wouldn't know two dudes were behind you, fucking around in the grass because the john bore only tiny air vents, no windows.

In the meadow, Whitey stood with his pants and his underwear cuffed around his furry calves. His legs were slightly spread. O'Keefe focused on the firm, hairy muscles of the best ass he'd seen, save for his own in the mirror. The two balls dangling visibly between Whitey's legs were as fat and loose as he expected, moderately furry, glistening with sweat.

Like his guess about the other cop's balls, O'Keefe was also correct about there being another man's mouth and asshole growing intimate with Whitey's dick. Though he couldn't see the culprit's face from the angle, his muscled right arm hung around Whitey's bare knee. Tons of ink. That handsome fucker with the buzzed scalp.

O'Keefe thought about coughing to clear his throat, but sensed that just about anything he did to announce his presence would lead to problems, endless explanations, and denial. Chaos. His cock refused to wait.

"You gonna give some of that to me?" he instead asked out loud, squeezing on his thickness on the march across those few final feet of meadow, to the prize.

As he suspected, the results were instantaneous, and almost disastrous. Whitey pulled his dick free from the dude's mouth, and O'Keefe heard the sloppy *plop* as contact between the men broke. The construction dude started up to his feet, but O'Keefe forced him back down with a hard shove on his shoulder. It was like trying to wrangle a hardened criminal, some felon used to being on his knees and breaking the law.

"No, stay where you are. You ain't done yet—my dick needs your attention."

O'Keefe yanked out his cock and one of his nuts, wagged them at the man's face. Tattooed dude tipped a look at Whitey, whose eyes, he guessed, were equally wide behind his silver shades.

"Do it," O'Keefe commanded and, at long last, the man's warm lips settled around his cock. "I've been getting the shit end of this detail all week. Time I enjoyed some of the same fun you've used to pass the time."

The tattooed dude showed O'Keefe's cock some affection, taking it as deep as possible without choking. Fresh perspiration poured. The musky stink of masculine flesh intensified. O'Keefe lifted to the tops of his toes before again going back down. Saying nothing, he placed a hand on the rookie's muscled abdomen. O'Keefe's fingers walked lower into Whitey's patch of blond curls. Lower yet. Whitey tensed.

"But—?" the rookie protested.

"Don't worry, dudes," O'Keefe said. "I'm good with all of this. *Great*, in fact."

Licking his lips, O'Keefe leaned down and guided Whitey's leaking cock into his mouth. The gamey taste of precome ignited on his tongue. Whitey grunted an oath under his breath. Veteran patrolman then tasted rookie balls, loving their ripeness. A few more deep sucks on Whitey's cock, and the look of shock on his face morphed into one of comfort. The secret duo was now a configuration of three.

And O'Keefe wanted in. Permanently.

Straightening, he said, "Hand it over."

"Hand over what?" Whitey asked.

"The skin. I know you dudes have some," he said, pulling his dick free and slapping it over the face of the dude down on his knees. "The condom. I've been tripping over your used junk all week."

Whitey reached into his pocket and pulled out a single foil packet.

"Go ahead, put it on," O'Keefe ordered.

While Whitey obeyed, O'Keefe brought Tattooed Dude up from his knees and tugged down his pants, baring an ass almost as magnificent as Whitey's. He planned to eat it to get it ready for the rookie's cock, would suck the other cop's balls some more, lick his asshole, too. And then while Whitey stuffed Tattooed Dude at one end, O'Keefe planned to fill the other. But first—

"We pull another detour detail together after this," O'Keefe said, lowering for that first lick into the sweaty heaven between the road-crew worker's muscled cheeks, "I get to be the one who bones his hole first."

"Deal," Whitey said, and O'Keefe feasted.

THE NIGHT I BLEW THE NEW BLUE

Eric Del Carlo

New-cop smell. Crisp blue uniform. Badge polished to a high gloss. I admit it...rookies are my weakness.

Maybe it was the wide-eyed eagerness or the purity of their desire to Protect and Serve. Or maybe I was sliding toward my forties with all those cop years under my belt, and the young ones just got my juices going. Whatever it was, when I got partnered with Damien Krantz, a blond-haired, blue-eyed jewel of a man, I knew I had to have him.

Even with my years on the job, I still drove a patrol car at night. As we headed out from the station house, Damien, blue eyes big in a sharp handsome face, asked me, "You don't want to do something else on the force?"

"What, sit at a desk?" I was driving.

"Sure. You've earned an easy assignment, haven't you?"

"This," I said, gesturing at the car and the nighttime city streets, "is what being a cop means to me. If I'm going to park myself behind a desk, I might as well sell insurance."

Damien grinned. It lit up his already attractive features. I kept peeking at him sidelong, with desire warming my gut, and my cock stirring in my slacks. He had no ring on his finger and hadn't mentioned a girlfriend.

I wasn't some aging, sad-sack letch, mind you. At thirty-nine, I stayed in just about peak physical form, with well-kept muscles and minimal fat on my six-foot-five body. Being in shape made the job easier, but it was also a matter of pride. I could still pick up nearly any guy I wanted at a bar.

Right now, though, I wanted this rookie.

Of course, there were rules about fraternization, and I wouldn't do anything to jeopardize my job or my partner. Still, Damien was irresistible. Even with my bent for newbies, this guy stood out as the ultimate prize.

After a couple hours of patrol, during which I sagely answered Damien's many questions about police work, I turned our car toward the park. It was a big two-block preserve, with dense stands of trees cut with paths. During the day it was a great place to take your family for a picnic. But at night, the city park was turned toward other, less wholesome purposes.

I nudged the car onto a path and crept it out onto the empty basketball court, where I parked.

"You go one way, I go the other," I told my twenty-five-year-old partner. "Walk the paths, shine your flashlight. You might see some things that'll startle your delicate sensibilities. Basically, we're just shaking the branches here. Don't get carried away."

"Okay, Harry. And my sensibilities aren't all that delicate."

We'll see, I thought as we got out and split up.

Park patrol was really Vice Squad shtick, but I hit this place about once a week. Personally I thought that what guys got up to among the trees at night was pretty harmless, but my occasional presence, I thought, kept the scene from getting out of hand. After all, nightly woodland orgies would spook the puritans.

So I walked one of the winding paths under the trees and made lots of scuffing noises, and now and then flicked on my flashlight. A couple of times I saw fleeting movement and bare skin among the dark greenery, as of people hastily grabbing their clothes and scampering out of sight.

After about fifteen minutes I made my way around to the other side of the park, where Damien would be meeting up with me. I waited, wondering with a quiet chuckle if he'd seen any of the male-on-male "shenanigans" and how he would react. If I was going to be honest, it was the real reason I'd brought him to the park tonight, so I could gauge his response.

I waited another minute or two, but he still didn't show.

Just before I grabbed for my radio, police instincts kicked in. I moved briskly down the unlit path, senses fully alert. Something told me that Damien was *not* in trouble, but I hurried to find him anyway.

I moved quietly, and after a couple of turns down the pathway I paused. Hearing something, I peered into the trees and bushes. Sure enough, about twenty yards off the trail a pair of anonymous male lovers were going at it. I could just glimpse where one leaned back against a tree trunk, his pants around his knees. The second man was kneeling and frantically bobbing his head. The wet slurping of his mouth carried on the night air.

Although this violated "decency" laws of public lewdness and all that, I found myself just staring for a moment, acknowledging the simple beauty of the act. These two men had no doubt first encountered each other minutes ago. Maybe they hadn't even traded any words, just gone into the brush by mutual silent agreement to satisfy their perfectly natural urges.

I crept a little off the path, still moving quietly. Leaves brushed my sleeves and cap. I wanted to see better.

The guy giving the blow job looked close to my age, with a little gray in his hair even, but with solid shoulders and a muscular frame from what I could see by the city light that made it through the foliage. He was deep-throating his lover with every plunge of his mouth, sucking right down to the man's balls, which he cupped gently. The blow job's lucky recipient was in his twenties, with spiky hair and a flat abdomen. His pretty features were contorted in pleasure, as his head rolled back and forth on the tree bark, mouth gaping and making soft little cries.

It was mesmerizing. I realized I had a blazing hard-on. I moved a few steps deeper into the trees.

The blow jobber sucked intently, his speed building, forcing the other's onrushing climax. I knew how it felt to take such control of another man's sexual responses. Sometimes when I sucked a guy off, it was like I owned him a little. I clearly saw the helpless ecstasy on the face of the twentysomething backed against the tree. He moaned louder.

Instinctively, I reached to rub myself through my blue slacks. Then, suddenly, I froze. I was aware of a presence close by, ahead on my right.

I saw it was Damien Krantz.

He too was watching the scene but was even more caught up in it than I. Damien had his cock out and was pumping himself at a steady rhythm, gasping breathlessly, blue eyes wide.

I felt shock. But it was followed by a raging tide of excitement. He hadn't noticed me, and I drank in the sight of his delectable cock as he worked it with his fist. His balls swayed enticingly. His pants were halfway down his thighs, and I beheld the lovely halves of his sculpted ass.

He must have sensed me, though, because he finally turned.

Those beautiful blue eyes just about popped out of his skull, and an awful look of guilt and fear came over him. I strode quickly to him, squeezed his shoulder, and whispered, "It's okay. There's nothing wrong with what you're doing." I felt a little like a kindly adult trying to console a kid who'd gotten caught jerking off.

I could feel Damien trembling. My sympathy for him was real. He might be thinking his career was on the line. I brushed his cheek with my fingertips.

"It's just…" he said, in a frail little hush. "Just…I remember—in college. These two guys I would watch from my dorm window. They'd go at it in their room every night. I always wondered, I always wanted…"

I didn't need any more of the story. My empathy only grew for my young partner, who'd never gotten to or allowed himself to act on his natural desires.

Leaning toward Damien, I grazed his cheek with my lips and said, "Go on watching those two while I suck you. You've waited long enough."

He went stock-still for a second then gave me a mute eager nod. I glanced once more at the lovers farther back in the bushes, seeing the older man working that cock, while the younger guy shuddered and groaned and thrust his hips at the devouring mouth. Both were far too preoccupied to notice us.

I slid to my knees in front of Damien. His hard-on had barely wilted. I took hold of his balls, feeling the warmth and size of the fleshy pouches. I inhaled his soapy-sweaty scent, gooseflesh rising on me, and my cock even dribbling a little in my pants. In the shadows I gazed at the glory of his full, veiny shaft.

The rookie was about to feel his first male mouth on his meat.

First I swirled his plum-like cockhead with my tongue,

feeling every smooth contour. Damien leaned back against the nearest tree to steady himself. His shoes crunched softly in the fallen leaves as he planted his feet. His undone belt creaked with the weight of his pistol. Having spit-buffed him, I sealed my lips around the crown of his cock and started swallowing my way down.

I was a practiced cocksucker, of course, but I still savored every delicious inch. My tongue plucked at his thick veins. I felt the throb of him as I caved in my cheeks around his shank. His balls stirred in my tender grasp. The ring of my mouth rode him down to his base. As that cockhead entered my throat, my nose buried itself in Damien's dark-blond curls. The bill of my uniform cap grazed his flat belly. I now had every bit of him in my mouth. His cock quivered delightfully inside me. I felt his whole body trembling against the tree.

For a second or two I just relished holding him like that. Then I set about giving him the overdue blow job he needed so badly.

My neck muscles settled into that familiar rhythm. My mouth stayed cinched tight around him, creating a sweet suction I knew he would appreciate. I withdrew up to the tip of him, then lunged back down, all the way every time. I deep-throated him mercilessly. I kept my teeth from grazing him and laved him with my skillful tongue. His manly flavor was thick in my mouth.

I couldn't help but imagine a young college-age Damien secretly watching those two dorm lovers, jerking off while he did it. With my free hand I undid my belt and yanked free my aching cock. I pumped myself, never flagging in my determined oral efforts. Damien deserved a great inaugural blow job, and I was goddamned well giving it to him.

He was helpfully jamming his cock into my mouth now. We worked at a cooperative tempo. I accommodated every hard

thrust of his hips. When his balls surged again in my hand, I
jerked my own meat harder. Suddenly, I felt him going taut and
heard the desperate gasp from above.

I pulled my mouth off him just as the hot spurts erupted.
Heavy droplets splashed the leaves beside me. I milked his balls
and smelled the luscious scent of his cum. I grinned. I hoped the
experience was as good as he must have fantasized it being all
these years.

Finally the last gush hit the ground, and he sagged back
against his tree. I stood, with my hard-on still lolling out of my
uniform slacks. And that, I figured, was how this night when I'd
blown the rookie—or "new blue"—was going to end.

But the night, I discovered, wasn't over yet.

I saw that the other pair of male lovers had progressed while
I'd been sucking Damien off. The younger of the two now had
his jeans around his ankles. He faced the tree, hugging it, as the
older man was giving it to him up the ass. I watched those fear-
some thrusts, gaping at the display. The older guy stopped to
tear away his sweatshirt, revealing a bare muscular torso. Even
in the cool air, his solid chest gleamed with sweat. A grin split
his face as he fucked that nicely molded ass.

Turning back toward Damien, I was about to mutter some
comment, but stopped short, stunned. My new young partner
had shed his uniform shirt, hanging it neatly from a branch,
and dropped his pants to the ground. He was holding a condom
packet toward me.

"Finish the fantasy for me, Harry," he said softly, then
stepped out of his slacks and hung them with his shirt. His
smooth lovely flesh seemed to glow beneath the trees. He turned
and thrust out his ass toward me.

I didn't let myself think. I hurried to tear open the condom
packet's foil, finding it was a pre-lubed job. Scrolling it onto my

quivering cock, I stepped in behind him. We didn't have much time. We were on duty and needed to get back to our patrol car. But I don't think there was much of anything that could have stopped me from guiding my latex-covered cockhead to that sweet youngster's waiting hole.

Rather than just jam myself into him, though, I took those extra courteous seconds and swirled my knob around his ring a few times, oiling him up with the condom's lube, and also giving him a chance to feel my size. If I was going to take his virgin ass, I wanted him to know what was—literally—coming.

But he turned his head and hissed over his shoulder, "Stick it in, damn it!"

So I planted my feet, set my cockhead flush to his ready hole, and started feeding my shaft into him. He pushed back against me, taking me deeper. I had my hands on his hips and felt his trembling reaction. "You okay?" I asked, wondering if I was hurting him.

"It's...so good. I dreamed about this for so long..."

It was all I needed to hear. I sank myself all the way in, loving how his channel gripped me like an eager fist. As when I'd been blowing him, the muscles of my body recognized this activity and settled into familiar patterns. Putting my weight forward on my toes, I set off stroking my cock into Damien's ass.

Pleasure rolled through me with every thrust. Heat churned in my gut as I plugged myself again and again into my new lover's innards. I gazed down in rapture at his naked body bent over in front of me. I felt like a sex-crazed jungle man out here with him, with the scent of nature all around and leaves falling on us in a faint night breeze.

I felt and heard the smack of my balls against the tense hemispheres of Damien's ass. Metal parts jingled on my belt. My breath felt tight in my lungs. Sweat stung my eyes. I fucked him harder, letting the mad speed of the act take over. No time to linger. I wanted to nail this ass until I shot my load. My body rolled and undulated and hammered against his.

My coming felt like it started at my feet, tightening my toes before working up my body in a rush. My knees shook. My hard thighs quivered. Then abruptly I was past the point of no return. The bliss boiled from my balls. I was jammed deep inside Damien as I started shooting jet after jet of cum into the condom, filling the latex sheath. My eyes rolled up into my head, and I had to dig my fingers into Damien's hips to keep from stumbling.

The delirium slowly receded. I stepped back, disengaging myself from my partner's no-longer-virginal asshole. I peeled off the condom. Disbelief whirled in me. Damien Krantz wasn't the first rookie I'd had during my long career, but I'd never done anything as crazy as this—fucking my new partner in a park on our first night.

I wanted to laugh hysterically. Instead, I stepped toward Damien as he reached for his clothes. He looked at me with wide blue eyes. "That was really special," I told him truthfully. Then I leaned in to kiss him, mindful if he wanted to pull back.

He didn't. He kissed me like a man, a proud man, with no regrets. I let him get his uniform back on while I tidied mine. I saw that the other lovers were gone, and wondered if we'd spooked them off. I hoped not. I hoped they'd gotten the chance to finish everything they had wanted to do under the trees.

When we both looked like respectable police officers again, Damien and I stepped back out onto the path and followed it to the car. The next night I asked him if he'd like to partner with me permanently.

BURNOUT

D. Fostalove

Detective Otis Moore strolled up the sidewalk toward the high-rise and entered the luxury condominiums' expansive lobby. He nodded at the security guard and the woman seated at the concierge desk and moved toward the elevators located near the back. He'd previously dealt with them the first time he'd been to the building looking to see if Isaac was home. He wasn't.

Exiting on the eleventh floor, Otis walked the carpeted hall to the last condo on the left and knocked lightly on the door. He wasn't looking for Isaac this time. He wanted to speak to the condo's owner. Waiting, Otis knocked again, before placing an ear to the door. Suddenly the door swung open.

"Can I help you?" a thick, dark-skinned man with long, crinkled locks asked. He had eyes the color of newly minted pennies that instantly captivated anyone who dared to stare into them.

Awestruck momentarily by the man's beauty and his unblinking eyes, Otis extended his hand. "I'm Detective Moore..."

"I've been expecting you." He stared at Otis's hand nonchalantly before looking up at him.

Otis thought to reach for his gun. Why would this man be expecting him unless he knew full well why Otis was visiting? "Have you?"

"Yes," the man said. "I heard you've been snooping around here. I'm not sure what you're looking for but whatever it is, it's not here."

"Are you Nate Davenport?"

"I could be," the man said with a shrug.

"I'd like to speak to you about Isaac," Otis said.

"Is he in some type of trouble?" The man inched forward and brought the door with him to prevent Otis from peeking inside.

"When was the last time you've seen him?" Otis wouldn't have asked a battery of questions standing in someone's doorway but figured this would be as far as the man would allow. Besides, this was his first real case as lead investigator. He would focus on honing his skills at a later date. Right now, he wanted to get to the bottom of things.

"Last Thursday night. I tossed him and some dirty dude with a pierced lip out," the man said without hesitation. "Any more questions?"

"Do you know where they went after leaving here?"

"No." The man waited for Otis to continue explaining the reason for his visit.

"Early Friday morning we found a car registered to him, a two-door coupe, on the south side behind a dilapidated gas station," Otis began. "It had been set on fire."

"I guess since I bought it, he would torch it to be spiteful," the man said. "I'm not surprised."

"Nate?"

"Yes?"

Otis continued. "There was a body inside, burned beyond recognition."

"What do you mean there was a body inside?" Nate's cautious demeanor instantaneously disappeared. He began rambling as thought after thought came to mind, each one more disturbing than the last. "Was it Isaac? Do you think he was murdered? You're not suggesting I had anything to do with it, are you?"

"No," Otis said. "I'm aware that you flew out to Miami that night and didn't return until early this morning."

"Tell me he wasn't inside."

Otis avoided eye contact. "Maybe you'd like to take a seat."

Nate's voice rose and became unsteady as he demanded to know if Isaac was inside. Otis stood frozen, unable to speak to the man, stunning even in distress. Nate turned suddenly and ambled toward a tan leather love seat.

"Dental records indicate the body belonged to a Francisco Herrera," Otis said, as he stepped inside and closed the door behind him. "Was that the man you referred to as having the pierced mouth?"

"Yes," Nate mumbled.

Otis hated being the bearer of bad news. Outside of viewing dead bodies sprawled in the street like trash, breaking the news of a loved one's death always brought him dread.

"If the body in the car was Cisco, what about Isaac? Where is he?"

"I was hoping you knew."

Seated on the sofa, Nate placed both hands over his face and shook his head in disbelief. Otis stepped forward and placed a hand on Nate's shoulder, while the man mumbled how he couldn't believe how something like this could happen. He wished he hadn't thrown Isaac out that night. He wanted to tell Isaac not to leave with the strange, fast-talking guy he said he'd met days before at some house party.

Nate moved both hands from his tear-streaked face. "What happened?"

"We are still piecing everything together," Otis said, being careful not to reveal too much. "We really need to find Isaac."

Nate wiped his face with the back of his hand and slumped deeper into the chair. "You suspect Isaac had something to do with...that's why you're here, right?"

Otis gave a canned response as he'd been taught. "He is a person of interest."

"Why? He could never do anything like that."

Otis started to mention how several anonymous tipsters had reported seeing the drunken pair barhopping and then arguing about Nate later outside a Waffle House, but he knew that divulging that much information would be a typical rookie mistake. He needed answers and hoped Nate would be able to provide him more insight than he already had.

"He's not a suspect at this point," Otis assured him.

Looking at Otis suspiciously, Nate continued wiping at his eyes. "Well, like I said, the last time I saw him was Thursday night before I left for the airport. He was upset because I told them to leave. He began cursing and then chucked his keys to the floor. I ignored his tirade and gathered my luggage. He and Cisco stormed out before wishing my plane would crash."

As Nate spoke, Otis scribbled down several details on his notepad. "Did you speak with him on the phone anytime after that?"

Nate shook his head. "We usually don't talk for days after an argument."

"You say he threw his keys down. I'm assuming you mean his keys to your home," Otis said. "Was he still living here then?"

"He would stay on the couch from time to time," Nate said, then paused, taking a moment to watch Otis as he jotted down something, "whenever his newest boy toy would put him out."

"Were Nate and Francisco seeing each other that you know of?"

"There's no telling." Nate stood and made his way to the kitchen where he grabbed a bottle of water from the fridge. He offered Otis one but he declined. "I knew no matter what man caught his eye, he'd always be back."

"Do you think he'll come back now?"

Nate stopped taking a drink from the bottle. "If he did what you suspect, he won't come back. He's not stupid enough to show his face around here with you and your cronies swarming."

Knowing there wouldn't be anything else he could gather from Nate, Otis reached into his pocket and retrieved a business card. "If he tries to contact you, will you give me a call?"

"What's in it for me?" Nate asked, before adding when it appeared Otis was thinking of a response, "It was a rhetorical question, Detective."

"I know," Otis said, his heart thumping.

"If he calls, I'll let you know."

Otis typed a potential suspect's street name into a criminal database on a new case he was working. He scrolled through several mug shots with attached rap sheets, and picked up the desk phone shortly after its initial ring. "Daytona Beach Homicide Unit, Detective Moore speaking."

"I have something you may be interested in, Detective," the man on the other end said.

Immediately recognizing the voice as Nate's, Otis perked up. He stopped scrolling, grabbed a pen and waited. "I'm listening, Nate. Go ahead."

Nate chuckled. "I didn't give you my name."

"You didn't need to." Otis nodded to a fellow detective as she walked by his desk.

"Isaac called late last night," Nate said. "He wanted to meet. We needed to talk, he said, but didn't say about what."

Otis frantically scribbled on his pad while questioning Nate about the number that showed up when Isaac called and whether he had said anything else during the call. Nate revealed they hadn't actually spoken because he never picked up the phone unless he recognized the number. He said the message had been left on voice mail. When Nate called the number back, a homeless man answered and informed him the number he had dialed belonged to a pay phone outside a liquor store off International Speedway Boulevard.

"Did he say where he wanted to meet?"

"He didn't have to. We have a spot on the beach...."

Otis waved over his senior investigator and pointed to the legal pad where he'd written Isaac's name and a quick message about him being in contact with Nate. The veteran investigator leaned against Otis's desk as he continued speaking. "Did you meet him?"

"No." Nate asked Otis to hold because someone was ringing on the other line.

The hairs on Otis's arms stood up. He knew it was Isaac. "Conference me in."

Waiting anxiously for Nate to merge the calls, Otis cupped a hand over the phone and whispered to the detective propped up on his desk. "I think the suspect in that torched car case just called our informant while we were on the phone."

Nate returned moments later, sounding drained. "That was him. He's scared."

"Did he say where he was?"

Nate hesitated before he spoke. "At a hotel. He wouldn't say which one."

Otis could tell Nate was lying. Nate knew, either by Isaac's outright admission or lack of a response when asked, that the man he'd loved had committed the heinous murder. Otis knew Nate was scared, upset and sad for his former lover. He was probably flooded with many other feelings Otis couldn't begin to imagine. Otis realized that although Nate had lied about Isaac's whereabouts, he hadn't called simply to talk about rainbows and unicorns. He'd called to provide a lead.

"Does he still want to meet?"

"Yes, at our spot when the sun goes down."

Otis took down the details of the men's special spot and hashed a plan to have several officers strategically placed in the immediate vicinity while Nate leisurely drove up and got out to meet Isaac. Otis explained that when Nate saw officers creeping from underneath the pier, he was to run in the opposite direction and around the beachside resort to safety. Nate reluctantly agreed, just as long as they didn't hurt Isaac in the process.

Emerging from the shadows as two officers hauled a screaming and cursing Isaac to an awaiting squad car, Otis approached Nate, who stood in the sand looking completely helpless. Otis's first instinct was to hug Nate and tell him the pain and feelings of betrayal would subside in time, but he quickly shook the thought from his head. Nate wasn't a grieving mother or child who had just been told their loved one was found dead in a gutter.

"What you did was very brave," Otis said.

When Nate noticed it was Otis who was speaking, he shook his head and turned away.

"Thank you for helping us solve this case."

"This isn't right," Nate said in a low voice. "I shouldn't have called."

"Yes, you should have."

"But why? To see my...him hauled away forever?"

Otis thought back to the training manuals that advised how to address citizens who informed the police of their family member's criminal misdeeds. "Whatever reason Isaac had for killing Francisco, he was still someone's son, nephew, uncle and friend. They deserve justice. Your assistance with our investigation was the right thing to do."

"Yeah, I guess," Nate said dryly as he walked by Otis. Otis let him go. He could tell how distraught Nate was over the whole episode.

"I'll be in contact...regarding the case."

Without glancing back, Nate said, "I've done all I can for you and your case."

Downing the rest of a cocktail, Otis set the glass on the bar and glanced up at one of several televisions showing a tennis match between Venus Williams and a woman whose name escaped him. As he followed the little neon ball flying from one side of the court to the other, Otis felt someone's presence behind his stool. Before he could turn, he heard the man's whisper.

"Is this seat taken, Detective?"

Otis hadn't imagined he'd ever see Nate again, although everyone seemed to bump into each other all the time in Daytona Beach. He was nearly an hour away though, in Saint Augustine, Florida. Friends, family and coworkers knew that after particularly taxing cases, he would sneak away to Saint Augustine to ease his mind in a different locale.

"Cat got your tongue?"

Before Otis could offer the seat or ask how Nate had found him, the man hopped onto the stool next to him. Otis glanced at the gold tank top hugging Nate's chest and immediately thought of a Mr. Goodbar. Oh how he wanted to reach over and peel away the wrapper to reveal the smooth, dark, nutty goodness inside. He averted his eyes, thinking everything about the scene was against the detective's code.

"I did a little investigative work myself. I think I did a pretty good job, don't you?"

"Yes, I do," Otis said while still keeping his eyes averted. "But why?"

"Why do we do half the things we do?"

When Otis didn't respond, Nate turned to the bartender and ordered a drink.

"Isaac prays I rot in the deepest pits of hell for betraying him."

"Sorry to hear that," was all Otis could think to say. He realized the alcohol had taken effect. He wasn't really sorry at all but rather pleased they'd caught Isaac; his first case as lead investigator had been solved succinctly.

"We weren't any good for each other anyway." Nate glanced up as Venus screamed and jumped about excitedly while spectators hooted and hollered. The bartender set a drink down in front of Nate. He stared at it for a moment before grabbing the straw and moving the ice cubes around in the drink.

"You're real quiet," Nate said after another stretch of silence between them. "You okay?"

"I'm all right." Otis wasn't in the mood to discuss his innermost thoughts, no matter how attractive the person asking it was. It wasn't like Nate would understand the burden that came with being a homicide detective anyway.

"You sure?"

"Yeah." Otis looked at Nate and saw what appeared to be genuine concern. "I'm a little tired, nothing major."

Nate nodded and looked into the nearly empty cocktail glass. Otis finished the rest of his drink and excused himself to go to the restroom; the liquor had gone through his system faster than usual. How many drinks had he consumed?

When he returned, Otis found Nate standing with a worn leather wallet in his hand. He tossed several bills on the bar before downing the rest of his drink.

"You're leaving?"

"I shouldn't have come all the way out here," Nate said as he stuffed the wallet back into his pocket. "I could've just called you at work and thanked you over the phone."

"Thank me for what?"

"Saving my life," Nate said just above the bar's rambunctious patrons. "I didn't know Isaac had the capacity to kill."

"You're welcome." He sat on the stool, hoping Nate would follow suit. He did not. He nodded and thanked Otis again before saying farewell.

"See you around."

"Don't leave," Otis screamed in his mind several times before his lips parted to release the words. They came out as a plea, but he didn't care. He wanted the company, needed *his* company.

Turning just as he reached the door, Nate said, "I should probably go. I don't know what I was thinking when I came all this way in the first place."

"I don't know either, but I'm glad you did." Otis was shocked at his words.

A slight smile crossed Nate's face. He slowly returned to his seat. "You look very nice outside your work clothes."

Otis was dressed down in khaki shorts, a light blue polo shirt and canvas shoes. His head was freshly shaven and his mustache trimmed. He nodded at the compliment and leaned in to whisper how attractive he had thought Nate was from the moment they'd met.

"Why didn't you say anything then?" Nate waved the bartender over to order again.

"I was on business."

Both men stole glances at each other before turning to the overhead television where Venus received the Rosewater Dish for her win over Marion Bartoli. As Otis watched the bar patrons celebrating Venus's win, he silently thanked the heavens for a second chance to be in Nate's presence, although he was exhausted from his job.

He glanced at Nate who was coolly sipping another drink. "Tell me something about you."

"Like what?" Their eyes met.

"Anything. I want to hear your story." Otis requested another drink. "How're you able to afford to live in such an upscale building as the Princeton on a school counselor's salary?"

"How'd you know I was...? Silly question, right?" Nate chuckled. "My dad's a drug dealer."

Otis's eyes widened as Nate shrugged nonchalantly while looking up at the television.

"Are you serious?"

"Yeah," he said before he burst out laughing. "I'm pulling your leg. It was a foreclosure."

The two spoke late into the night, laughing over funny child-hood stories, reminiscing about torrid love affairs and sharing what they aspired to do with the rest of their lives. They chatted until they realized they were the only two left at the bar.

Not wanting their time together to end, the men decided to continue hanging out at the resort Otis had booked for the weekend a couple of blocks away. Laughing and stumbling out of the bar from the half-dozen drinks they'd consumed throughout the night, they made their way down the road and eventually to the eighth floor beachside suite.

Otis closed the door behind them while Nate ambled through the sitting room with aid of the wall and practically fell into the bed. They burst out laughing as Otis walked to the mini-fridge to retrieve a bottle of water.

"Come out onto the balcony with me. We can watch the sunrise together if we stay up long enough," Otis said.

"We can watch from here." Nate scooted farther onto the bed and patted the spot next to him. "Do I have to make myself any clearer?"

Although tempted, Otis insisted they chill on the balcony and enjoy the balmy breeze blowing off the ocean. When Nate didn't budge, Otis moved the vertical blinds aside and pulled the sliding door open, allowing the breeze to blow into the room. He hoped it would entice Nate to join him. Nate responded by pulling his tank top off and propping himself up on several pillows. Once again he patted a spot on the bed and smiled.

"I really want to watch the sunrise."

Nate climbed from the bed and trudged across the floor toward the balcony. "You win...for now."

They sat in the pair of wicker chairs angled toward each other and stared into the darkness, hearing the waves crash against the beach. Otis opened the bottle of water he still held and chugged it down before placing the empty container on the floor.

"Whenever I start feeling burnt out, I drive out here and book a beachside room," Otis said. "Watching the sun rise and set always soothes me."

"I hear you, but all I'm thinking about is kissing you right now," Nate said.

"Really?" Otis turned to see Nate staring at him.

"Yes, really."

The alcohol had eased Otis to the point where ethics didn't matter. No one had to know about what two grown men did after bumping into each other in another city. How would anyone know Otis had previously worked with Nate to solve a murder case?

As if reading Otis's mind, Nate got up and moved to where Otis was slouched in his chair. He leaned down and kissed Otis. Otis reached his left hand up and wrapped it around the back of Nate's neck, bringing him in for a more passionate, prolonged kiss. Nate tugged at Otis's polo shirt, hoping he would take it off. Otis obliged.

Both bare-chested, Nate knelt between Otis's legs and began tonguing one of his nipples while playing with the other with his thumb and index finger. Otis bit his lip and looked toward the sky, realizing it had started to lighten. He let out a sigh and closed his eyes. His hands came to life then, finding their way to Nate's crinkled dreadlocks. He ran his fingers through their softness, subtly pushing Nate's head toward his throbbing erection.

"You want me to go lower?" Nate asked, while tonguing Otis's other nipple.

"Yes."

Nate planted kisses down Otis's stomach as his hands unbuttoned Otis's khaki shorts. As Nate tugged, Otis squirmed out of the shorts. With Otis's erection throbbing under his chin, Nate opened his mouth and took the thick rod in as he worked to remove Otis's shoes. As he continued sucking, Nate played with Otis's bare feet. He moved his hands along Otis's arches, cupped his heels and intertwined his fingers with the toes.

Otis was so caught up in the thoroughness of Nate's mouth, he hadn't realized that Nate had unzipped himself and began rubbing his dick along the contours of his foot. He kept playing in Nate's hair as his head bobbed up and down.

"Deep-throat it. Just like that."

Nate swallowed all of Otis before releasing him. He backed into the balcony's railing and lifted one of Otis's legs, placing a foot in his mouth while he began masturbating himself. Surprised at how turned on he was at seeing Nate suck his toes, Otis grabbed his dick and began jacking it. He grabbed his nipple with his free hand and moved his other foot up and down Nate's chest.

Hungrily, Nate grabbed the other foot and inhaled it while he pulled at his dick. Otis wiggled his toes in Nate's mouth while Nate reached between them and began playing with Otis's balls as he continued jacking himself.

As Otis noticed the blinding orb appear to rise from the water, he felt himself about to climax. He stared beyond the balcony at the sun's rays shimmering in the ocean. The rays, sparkling like precious stones, mimicked the intensity between his legs. He kept pumping when he heard Nate howl. Otis focused on him as white globs erupted from between his legs, droplets landing on his shins, thighs and Nate's chest.

Otis convulsed in the chair as he began to orgasm too. Nate released his foot and buried his head into Otis's lap, eagerly sucking. Otis leaned his head back and let out a deep sigh. He felt himself coming down Nate's warm throat. He panted loudly as his heart pounded in his ears.

"Damn, that was good," Otis said, as he slumped farther into the chair. Absentmindedly, he asked, "What now?"

"What do you mean 'what now'?" Nate climbed to his feet and made his way to the other wicker chair. "We go to sleep, wake up, do it again, shower, find something to eat, come back and do it again. How's that sound to you?"

"Sounds like a plan." Otis closed his eyes, allowing the warmth of the sun to wash over him.

NEW DICK

Salome Wilde

Every new dick's got to have a first day in the office, a first time he plants his hindquarters in a chair assigned to him that's already had grooves worn into it by a guy who was once fresh like him. He knows damn well who sat in it and that the scuffs on the floor under the desk usually came from dead man's boots. Sure, the suit may be new, the gun a different make. But every new dick knows he's part of a game of cops and robbers that started before him and will go on long after he's gone. And maybe that's just how he likes it. Unless his first day is his last.

The day I joined the plainclothes clan on the second floor of the Sixteenth Precinct, I was proud. I had plenty of training, and I'd more than paid my dues as a uniform, on a beat most guys wouldn't walk if you paid them double overtime. But none of that counts once you're a suit, a real dick among dicks. The other guys looked at me like I was fresh off a cabbage truck, looks so cold I nearly froze on the spot. And my partner, one Joseph Densch, made clear that no one could replace his partner

Eddie—killed on the job when some wise guy popped him, three
bullets in the gut—and I shouldn't even try. I played it off, took it
in stride. Of course he'd feel that way. Joe pushed, though, giving
me the third degree about the difference between brains and
brawn, and how Eddie had both. When I kept my cool, he gave
me a stony glare and turned to talk to his buddies as if I wasn't
there, complaining about how the "new mugs" they sent up were
too young, too dumb, too ugly. I laughed: I was just a guy doing
a job, a job I'd earned. As for ugly, I said, I fit right in.

The others seemed to like me a little better after that—or at
least they left me alone. Joe, meanwhile, took off. Off to avenge
his partner's death, he said, and he sure as hell didn't want a
punk like me along. "Best way to end up dead myself," he said.

I shrugged that off, too. What else could I do? The chief
hadn't given us a case yet. I decided to just make myself at
home. The coffee was lousy, but it was coffee. The desk had
been cleaned out, mostly, but I pushed around my stapler and
paper clips and found a replacement bulb for the rusty lamp that
gave my notepad a sickly yellow glow. I doodled bean shooters
in the margins.

The next sight I saw was prettier than the sleekest weapon
I could imagine. The clack of shiny shoes on our dingy floor
turned all heads toward a tall, perfectly dressed figure with
porcelain skin, shiny auburn hair covered by a hat cocked at
a dangerous angle, and a green-eyed gaze so sharp you could
cut yourself on it. The room fell silent as the stranger walked
straight to my desk and sat down on the corner of it. "You
Eddie?" the sultry piece asked, giving me the once-over.

I shook my head. "Dead."

The eyes bore into me, checking for truth, and then they
dropped. Neatly removing the designer hat, the stranger
smoothed back a head of thick, wavy hair. A lock fell across the

fine-boned face. I itched to push it back in place. "Can I help?"

A nervous foot tapped. Those shoes alone were worth a month's salary and more to me. "Not here," came the reply.

I rose, catching the eyes of every lug in the room. *Eat your hearts out*, I thought, escorting the class act from the building.

With the sky still giving us the waterworks, we went into the coffee joint a few doors down. Having shifted precincts as part of the promotion, I couldn't know whether Daisy's Downtown Diner would offer a decent cup of joe, but it had to be better than what the lunks upstairs brewed for themselves. With its dingy booths and questionable angle on clean, I was sure it couldn't cook up a bite worthy of that wide, curved mouth or those manicured nails. We sat down anyway, and I ordered a couple of coffees. When I lit up a Lucky Strike, a hand reached across the table to take it from my lips. I grinned and gave way.

As I lit another, smoke and a refined voice floated over to me. "It's like this," the stranger began. "My lover is trying to kill me." It was one hell of a starter. "A 'friend' told me to ask for Eddie at the Sixteenth Precinct," the story continued. "I didn't know he was dead."

I nodded, taking a hefty drag off my butt. Those soulful eyes went right through me, so I was glad when the waitress clunked two steaming cups down between us. Had to keep my wits about me, I knew. The silence stretched. "What makes you think you're in danger?" I prompted.

A perfect eyebrow arched, the green eyes darkened. The shift was subtle, but I didn't get my promotion for missing cues. The wheels were clicking fast and hard in that minx's brain, deciding what to say and how to say it. A pointed tongue darted, gave a quick trace across even white teeth, and withdrew. Something inside told me I shouldn't trust a single word out of that mouth, now or ever, but I couldn't help wanting to hear every word it said. From the hokey story that was coming to the imagined sound of my name whispered low in a hotel bed, I was all ears.

"Look," the lies began, strong fingers wrapping the chipped coffee cup, "I don't know you and you don't know me, but I can tell you're the kind of guy who helps a person in trouble. And I'm in trouble, real trouble." The lips closed tight. I could see the jaw muscles working. Were those pretty peepers about to leak?

"What makes you think your lover's a threat?" I repeated, keeping my voice calm and professional. I might've been lured, but I wasn't gonna be suckered.

With a quick tug, the scarf that covered a smooth, pale throat was pulled away. I'd have been imagining my lips against that skin if that silk hadn't been covering some serious bruises. Though it was covered again almost as quickly as it was revealed, it sure seemed to my eyes like someone had taken a chokehold on that neck. I puffed hard on my stick and nodded my understanding.

"There's other evidence, but I can't show it here." We bumped knuckles as we stubbed our butts in the small, dirty ashtray between us. The touch was electric. We both mumbled apologies.

"So what'd you do to get the plug so riled up?" I asked, giving the tough cop voice. It would be easy to fall for this one. I had to turn the tables if I was gonna get the lowdown and not a runaround.

Those big eyes flashed fire, but I could take the heat. "He's a damned sadist."

If ever anyone "spat" words, those words were spat. But when I didn't respond, just sipped cheap joe and watched, the message that I wanted more, a lot more, was received.

"All right, so maybe he caught me with another guy. It's not like we were married, Mr...."

"Colter," I answered, "Reg Colter. You can call me Colt."

The auburn head gave a nod. "Colt. I like that."

I doubted a little game on the side was the full story, but jealous Brunos were a dime a dozen in this town. Likely there was some stealing or other dirty dealings along with the two-timing, but whatever there was, this looker didn't deserve to be roughed up, and especially not bumped off. A guy who couldn't control his lover was a sap in my book, and one that used force to make up for weakness was dirt. I pushed away my cup and met that green-eyed gaze on the level. "What do you want me to do?"

The sliver of a smile I got in reply was worth the price of admission. It made me tight in the trousers and then some.

"Come to my place tonight at eight," mouthed those inviting lips, slipping a little piece of paper into my hand with an address on it. "You can hide in the closet, and when Frank comes home— he usually gets in about nine—if he tries anything funny, you'll catch him right in the act." Sliding out of the booth and turning to go, the dish added in a husky whisper, "Don't forget your handcuffs."

I was hard as granite now, both of us knowing the stakes. If I busted this jerk, I'd reap the rewards. And I wanted them. "Hey," I called before the diner door closed. "I don't know your name."

"Craig," the babe answered, flashing me a real smile. "Craig Random."

The rest of the day in the office was worse than dismal. The guys had lunch brought in but "forgot" to include me. The smell of roast beef on rye with sour pickles made my gut rumble, but I shut it up with some peanuts from the penny machine in the lobby and kept focused on the night ahead. So what if Joe never

came back and I didn't even have papers to push around. I had
tonight to take my mind off everything else. In my first twenty-
four hours as a plainclothes dick I was gonna catch and bag a
bum in the act, rack up points with the chief and claim a tasty
reward from the doll of my dreams.

With the sun finally sinking behind the grimy office window,
I was sprung. I followed the few who actually stayed the full
shift down and out into the windy New York evening. Nothing
penetrated, even with my trench coat unbuttoned. I was numb
to the cold, deaf to parting jibes, blind to the litter in the gutter
and even the drunks begging for change as I hightailed it back
to my apartment. Once there, I downed some leftover chop
suey, knocked back a beer and smoked a couple of Luckys as I
listened to the radio. At seven, I took a shower to keep me fresh
for the action ahead—both the arrest and the reward Craig
Random was likely to give me after. Neither of my suits was
clean, but I made do with a shot of cologne and a change of
everything underneath.

At 7:24, I stood on the curb, hailing a cab, blowing smoke
into the chilly night air. It didn't take long to get a ride, and I
ignored the cabbie's chat, just giving a grunt every now and then
until he cheesed it. My mind was racing, skipping the time I'd
spend waiting and the confrontation itself, heading right for the
moment after we slammed the door behind the uniforms taking
my first collar to the local precinct where he'd be booked on
attempted murder. I couldn't wait to crush my mouth against
Random's, feel that hint of stubble, grip his hair and smell that
pricey tonic on my fingers, grind my hips against his to find
him as hard as I was, then lie back on the bed and watch as he
showed me every inch of what he hid under that swanky suit.
I shuddered and told the P.I. in my pants to relax as we pulled
up to the address. I didn't want to waste time counting pennies

and ended up tipping the cabbie more than I should have, but what the hell. Everyone should be as lucky as I felt.

Random answered the buzzer in a low, anxious voice and let me in. It was a lush place in a ritzy neighborhood: the hallway was wide and bright, the stairs were carpeted and it even smelled nice. I knew I'd link that scent of wood-oil soap and something flowery with Craig Random for the rest of my days. I clenched my jaw as I made my way up to 3B, and knocked twice. I thought I was prepared for seeing that high-class looker again, but I knew when he opened the door that I wasn't.

In the half-open doorway was a fantasy come to life. Random stood there like a Greek god in nothing but a plush white robe. His hair was damp, curling over his forehead and around his ears. He was rubbing it with a thick towel. The robe was short, and I openly admired his muscled calves. "Come in," he beckoned with a smile. As he turned and began to walk away, I couldn't help but take in those broad shoulders, that narrow, belted waist, and the shift of a small, tight ass under the robe.

He stopped and opened a closet, and then brought his strong, manicured fingers to wrap around me from behind. He felt for my gun, made a pleased little sound when he found it, and eased me out of my coat. I was dizzy. Random spoke as he hung up my trench and slipped my shoulder holster off. "I'll put this in with your coat. You can grab it when you're hiding in here. As soon as Frank rings the buzzer." I was about to interrupt, wondering why Frank wouldn't just use his key, but Random answered before I could ask. "Don't worry, Colt, I made sure he 'forgot' his key this morning," he said.

I loved hearing my name when he said it, that broad mouth so inviting. I nearly lost my cool and grabbed him right there. But Random had that covered, too. "He called half an hour ago. Said he's going to be late. I hope you don't mind." He walked slowly over to the sofa, and then sat, crossing his legs and exposing a juicy, muscled thigh. His robe parted a bit at the neck, too, and I took in the sight of that handsome chest with just the right amount of hair. He patted the cushion beside him. "Come on, detective, take a load off."

That was enough to make me give up any attempt at self-control. I wanted this luscious baby, and he was offering. I would get mine now, and Frank would get his later. I opted to stand, placing myself in front of Random and straddling his legs. Then I bent down and threaded my calloused fingers through that thick damp hair and tugged his head back. The sound he made—a sweet blend of surprise and arousal—was just what I wanted to hear as I kissed my way up his bruised throat to his parted lips. A tang of red wine clung to his breath as I crushed my mouth against his, forcing him to open to me and give as good as he got. I fed him tongue and he took it, sucked and licked it, and shared his own. It was sweet and hot, everything I imagined it would be.

Pretty soon I felt his hand working at my belt. I liked my lovers eager, so I didn't discourage his efforts. I yanked his hair a little harder, kissed him deep and long until he moaned a little and I felt my cock stiffen. Random released it with the skill of a professional. I grunted my approval into his mouth, and then broke the seal, standing up to look down on his nimble fingers around my hard shaft. Random was smiling, mischief in those irresistible eyes. "You like it?" I asked.

"I do," he cooed, squeezing a little then pulling down to slip my foreskin back. "Let me show you how much." Before I could reply, those soft, moist lips covered my sensitive, leaking head with a perfect kiss, and then he began to take me in, a tongue-tip teasing the slit and making me shudder.

"Damn," I groaned, and that just drove Random on, swirling

that soft tongue around and sliding slowly, inch by inch, down my achingly rigid cock. I brought a hand to his hair again and took a handful, guiding but not forcing him. This trick knew what he was doing, and I wanted to enjoy it just as it came. Still, a little tug of encouragement brought a sweet hum that ramped up the ride. A lesser stiff would've shot his load by now, but not me. This Colt was wild, an animal in his prime. "Suck it, sweetheart," I commanded, and he did.

After a while, I decided it was time to fulfill the fantasy I'd envisioned in the cab on the way over. I wanted to see more of Craig Random, to have him bare every inch of that handsome body for me and then take every inch of me inside. I pulled out of his mouth, taking in his flushed, swollen lips and brushing a thumb across a drop of sweat making its way down his cheek. "You're on fire, baby," I told him, and then licked the salty pad of my thumb.

"Some like it hot," he murmured, extending a hand to have me lift him to his feet. He buttoned my pants and escorted me to the bedroom, which was bigger than my whole apartment. When he flicked on the light, I took in the huge bed, draped in silk sheets and a thick comforter of baby blue.

"Nice," I said, approving of the surroundings. But Random himself was the centerpiece, standing before me, loosening his belt as I watched, and then letting his robe slip from his shoulders and down onto the polished hardwood floor. "Very, very nice," I added.

He lowered his eyes and gave a kind of shrug, a demure gesture that seemed as fake as a three-dollar bill, but sent all the blood rushing down to my already hard prick. He turned away to walk to the bed, and I couldn't have looked away for all the tea in China. Craig Random was a ripe, sensual Adonis, and mine for the taking.

I came to the side of the bed where he'd stretched himself out and undressed as fast as I could. He gave a low, playful chuckle at my eagerness, but nothing could slow me down now. He lay back as I climbed over him, and I ground our bodies together as he wrapped strong arms around my shoulders and legs around my hips. We kissed and ground into each other, and I couldn't resist bringing a hand down to press our shafts together and stroke. His eyelids fluttered closed, and I watched his changing expression as he grew firmer and began to leak into my grip. I leaned up to take a peek, and though I wasn't the type to admire a fella's meat, Random was absolutely prime cut.

His eyes opened and he released his grip when I shifted, twisting to reach the night table and pull open a drawer. I kept pumping us as he took out a little bottle and rolled back, humping into my hand and beginning to pant as he handed it to me. This dish thought of everything. When I let go, he spread his legs wide. I was used to giving it from behind, but as I lubed myself and he rolled his hips under, I couldn't resist slicking up my fingers and enjoying all he was offering. He took hold of his own cock and worked it prettily, while I watched and rubbed slippery fingers around that tight little hole. My dick ached, wanting in. But waiting was good, too, as I pressed inside just a little with one finger and then two. He gasped and shivered, and I pulled out, poured out a little more from the bottle, and dove in again. Soon, he was moaning with need and I was fucking him good and hard with my fingers, driving in as he matched my rhythm, stroking his pink-tipped cock, looking ready to burst. "Please," he whispered, and I withdrew my fingers to give him the real thing.

I nestled my way between his thighs and lined myself up. We locked gazes as I pressed forward, pushing in past that tight band of muscle that was no match for my need. Feeling generous,

I took hold of his cock as I gave him mine, and leaned in to kiss him as I drove into his firm, beautiful body. I had to will myself not to give way right then. Random's hot, tight, perfect ass was squeezing me so hard I felt like a teen again, giving my first fuck to the captain of the football team. "Give it to me," Random begged when I slowed to regain control, and I knew I had to oblige. Disappointing the doll was not an option.

He pulled his knees back as I drove in, faster and harder, jerking his cock in rhythm as best I could. I grunted as he whimpered and moaned, and we stayed in perfect sync, suspended in time. We were both close, I could feel it, but we fought off the finish together, determined to draw out every sweaty second of pleasure as long as we could. "You're so good," Random panted.

Voice rough, throat dry, I answered, "I know, baby, I know." And then he blew. Hands clawing my back, muscles locked and cock swollen, Random soared—and I was there to catch him. He sprayed his chest with thick white cream as I watched, his eyes wide, crying out in ecstasy. His body shook and his ass tightened so hard around my cock I had to cry out, too. I'd never seen a sight like it and couldn't get enough. Those parted lips and thick-lashed eyes, locked on mine. That mass of unkempt hair spread across the pillow. That flawless alabaster skin caressed by softly curling hair. That slender, slackening prick, still dripping seed. The man brought out the beast and the poet in me, and I felt him trembling and contracting around and beneath me as I thrust and thrust and came and came and came.

"Shit," Random suddenly gasped. We'd been lying, Random in my arms, catching our breath and contemplating round two, when the buzzer went off. It was Frank, home earlier than expected. I jumped up, instincts and adrenaline kicking in, and threw on my clothes while Random slid into some slacks and wiped off his chest. "Hurry," he said, rushing us out of the room and closing the door behind us.

We were both nervous, but I told Random I'd handle everything and I meant it, now more than ever. "Don't worry, baby," I said, giving Random a quick kiss as we headed into the front hall and I slipped into the closet.

The buzzer sounded again and Random pressed the button, trying to catch his breath. "Sorry, I was...washing up," he said softly. His voice made my blood curdle. It was fake, demure, a hint of fear behind it. I'd make sure he never had to use that tone again.

I couldn't see Frank when he came in because the closet opened away from the door. I tried to peek between the hinges, but it was no good. I'd have to be patient, wait for the sounds of a struggle. And, as it turned out, that wasn't long.

"You been drinking?" Frank's sour voice demanded.

"Just a glass of wine," Random answered, lightly.

I had my gun in hand, cocked and ready. I heard the sound of Frank's shoes, clicking down the hall, Random padding after. I looked out, but they were quickly disappearing into the living room. I didn't like it, but there was nothing I could do.

"Someone else been here?" Frank probed. I wondered what had given me away.

"Of course not," Random answered, all innocence.

"Then let's get to business," he said. I wondered what he meant, but there was no time for thought when I heard the sounds of a scuffle. I couldn't see what was going on, and my heart was racing.

"Don't," Random grunted. Then, in a high, panicked voice, "Stop Frank, don't!"

That was it. I swung the closet door wide and ran for the living room. Random and Frank were in a clench. Some kind of struggle was going on, but I couldn't make it out.

"What the hell!" Frank cried, trying to turn around when he heard me coming, but Random wouldn't let him.

"Shoot!" cried Random. "Shoot!"

And I did.

The next moments were like something out of a bad movie as Random let go and Frank's body slumped to the floor. There were two holes in his back. I watched the blood soak through his suit and pool over the Oriental rug I hadn't noticed until that moment. All my thoughts had been on Random. Though my training said I shouldn't touch the body, I knew I had to find the gun that would prove I'd shot to stop a murder. I tugged an arm and flipped him onto his side. There was no gun. Not even a knife. When I let him go and looked up, I found there was no Random either.

"Random," I called, keeping my gun out and hoping against hope I was wrong about what I suspected. The bedroom door was open again, and I headed in. Maybe Random had taken the weapon and just couldn't handle the sight of his abusive lover, dead on the floor. It hadn't done me much good either.

"Craig," I said, finding the room empty. The comforter still showed the imprints of our bodies. I turned at a sudden sound of clanking metal. I ran to the window and pulled back the drapes to see Random, a briefcase in his hand, jumping off the first-floor landing of the fire escape into the alley below. He blew me a kiss and jumped into a waiting cab. I'd been had.

In a daze, I dialed the Eighth Precinct and had them put in a call to the local cops and another to the chief. Sitting down on the sofa, I lifted the glass of wine Random had left behind and brought it to my lips. It was bitter. I waited in silence, listening for the sound of sirens. My first day as a dick would be my last.

THE
HORNINESS
TEST

Martha Davis

I t was my favorite road, long and winding, and I often took it because normally at this time of the morning I was the only soul using it. If your foot rides the gas petal a little extra hard and there's no PD to aim their speed guns in your direction are you technically speeding? No sooner had the thought formed—fucking blue lights!

Not again. Not now. He made me wait on the shoulder for a good ten minutes with said blue lights blinking away in my rearview mirror, slowly kicking the last pebble off the precipice of my temper. Fuck! And the thought of a speeding ticket on graduation night from the academy wasn't making the steel-enforced hard-on I'd been sporting for most of the night go away, either. Then the lights went dark and his silhouette exited the patrol car and walked toward me while I longed for the eighth-grade math book that I used to hide behind in my hot-for-teacher days.

"Boy, are you aware you're going seventy-five miles an hour in a fifty-five zone?"

I looked up into his light-blue eyes. *Boy? He planned to ride me hard.* "Probably."

"Care to tell me why?"

"You wouldn't understand."

"Try me."

"Well, Officer"—I decided to play civilian and not acknowledge his rank even though I knew full damn well what it was—"Let's just say I've spent the last couple of hours watching a batch of hot-ass male strippers bump, grind and gyrate in ways I'm sure their mommas didn't teach them as a way to celebrate my becoming one of you now."

"This excuse I must hear more about. Please continue."

He wants a good dirty story? I'll play. "Anyways, now I'm so horny I can't take it anymore. If I don't get home and wear out my hand or anything else I can find there, I won't be responsible for my actions. Do you need descriptions of that, too?"

"I see. Get out of the car."

"What?"

"You heard me. Get out of the car."

"Why?"

"You appear to be driving while horny. In fact, you just confessed and I need to administer a horniness test to confirm it."

A horniness test? Yeah, I shot him a totally disrespectful look.

"If I have to say get out of the car again, it's going to involve handcuffs."

He wouldn't dare! But then again, he just might. I opened the door to my Escalade and stepped out. Before I could get my second foot on the ground he yanked me by the elbow and pulled, slammed my door and threw me against it. His meaty arms forced mine into the small of my back and his thick thigh came up between my legs and parted them. I was pinned up against my truck like a bug.

The officer asked, "Can you identify what I have pressed against that tight bubble-ass of yours?"

"It's a big, fucking state-patrol dick," I replied.

"And what's it doing there?"

"It's growing bigger and harder with every breath."

I wiggled in his airtight embrace, crushing my ass into his black-uniform-covered crotch.

"And what does that big, hard dick make you want to do?"

"It makes me want to get on my knees and suck it."

"That's all? Coming from a city rookie ballsy enough to mouth off to an experienced state-patrol officer, I expected more."

He nibbled on my ear, pressed kisses down the side of my throat then worked his way to the base where he licked and blew air on the wet skin, making me tremble in his embrace. He sucked that same spot so hard I growled and arched my back against his stone frame, trying to get closer to his mouth.

Damn, he was giving me a hickey, putting a claim on my neck I didn't think my uniform could hide in the morning.

He whispered into my hair, "What else do you want to do to my cock, boy?"

"I, uh, want to suck it."

"You said that already."

"I want you to fuck my face, bury my nose in your groin hair and test my gag reflexes."

"You are too focused on sucking my dick. Get down there and do it until you can be creative and come up with something better."

"Here? On the side of the road?"

"Right here's where you said you wanted to suck my dick, so right here's where you'll suck it."

He spun me around with such strength I felt like a rag doll. I wasn't a small man, maybe two inches shorter and fifteen pounds lighter, but up against him like this, I felt beta. His hands grasped my shoulders and pushed hard, so hard I had to clutch his arms at the elbows to balance and make the drop to my knees smoother.

While working the fastenings of his gun belt and pants, I looked up into his face. Even in the dark of early morning, the moon reflected in his sky-blue eyes, the almost orange of his Marine-buzz-cut red hair, the bridge of freckles sprinkled across his nose. So sweet, so boyish, so Opie Taylor. But this was one of the strongest men I'd ever fucked. Even more than the occasional bodybuilding stripper I used to sample in the storage rooms at the club where I worked before I joined the academy. This officer's strength came from use, not show. When the streets got tough, he had to be strong. His life depended on it.

As I slid his pants and boxers down to midthigh, his cock stood up straight and hard. I stroked it with my hand while I buried my nose in his balls. He smelled like fuck; he was catnip for horny rookies.

I licked his fuzzy balls and took turns sucking them into my mouth, first the left, then the right. He groaned and thrust deeper into my face, cramming my chin into his inner thigh. He put his index finger under my jaw and lifted my face, removed my hand from his dick and aimed it at my lips.

His dickhead penetrated my lips and I licked it, loving the taste of warm, salty cop. My hands clutched the cheeks of his ass and I went down farther, sucking so hard his dick made a loud pop when it exited my mouth.

"Again," he grunted, and thrust back into my open mouth.

I gave everything I had to licking and sucking the thick girth of his dick with his hand braided in my black curls, holding my head in place while he thrust his way closer to completion.

A call came across the radio on his belt, one he had to respond to, and I jerked away, reminded of where I was and what I was doing.

When he finished talking, he put the radio up on the roof of the Escalade.

"It's all right. Keep sucking, Seth." He caressed my cheekbone gently and tried to penetrate my mouth again, but I didn't want to play this game anymore.

"No. We'll get caught. We're on the damn side of the road. A deserted road, but there's a chance someone could come this way. It's not worth the risk."

"Both of us need a good fuck too bad to stop now."

I clutched his arms and used them to climb the length of his body. At my full height, I took his jaw in my hands and kissed him as quickly and sweetly as I could.

"We'll continue this at home." I kissed him again, not wanting to stop but feeling I had no other choice. "My hard dick isn't going anywhere."

"Oh, we are doing this. Here and now."

I used to be the brazen one. Somewhere along the way we switched roles, and he became the one who flipped his middle finger at the discretion I sought. Did becoming a cop really change me that much?

The moonlight glistened in his eyes giving them a naughty twinkle.

"Go over to the passenger side of your truck. Even if someone drives by they won't see anything." He pulled his pants back up but did nothing to refasten them, and he had to hold them up with his left hand because the weight of his belt threatened to drop them again.

I thought about how discreet we could really be, even behind my Escalade, parked on the shoulder in front of a cop car. It would be begging a rubbernecker to slow down and take a peek, but I followed along when he led me around my truck, and when I opened the front passenger door he said, "I know you have some lube in here somewhere."

I reached in, opened the glove box and pulled out a half-full bottle of KY. After his, "That's a good boy," I replied, "So you want me to fuck you?"

"No, I'm going to fuck you. It's my turn."

"That's not the way I remember it."

"Well, I'm the one with the handcuffs, so that makes you my bitch."

Charlie pushed me down and pinned my chest into the passenger seat with his left hand while his right worked at opening my fly. He took my dick and stroked it hard, making me groan into the seat leather.

"Hand over the lube, boy." His return to hardcore cop was complete.

We wrestled over it and eventually I "accidentally" lost my hold on the bottle and surrendered. He popped the top with his teeth and poured lube onto his dick, smearing it over his entire length, and my asshole, then put the bottle on the roof. Instead of testing me with his fingers first, he used the head of his dick, pushing through my sphincter. Once he had broken that barrier, with each thrust I could feel him going deeper and deeper. He kept me pinned to the seat with one hand while he used the other to stroke my cock to the same rhythm with which he was fucking me.

"I'm going to come in your ass, boy. What do you think about that?" he grunted.

"Please! I need it bad!"

I begged for his come until his rhythm grew erratic and his hips jerked. With a loud grunt he filled me with a week's worth. I took my own dick out of his hand and finished myself off, coming from between my legs on his fancy cop shoes.

"Oh, you're going to pay for that." He laughed and leaned in to press a kiss between my shoulder blades.

Last summer, I met Charlie at the club where I worked as a bartender. It was my last night. I had finished my two weeks' notice and would be up first thing that morning to start my first day at the academy. I caught him checking out my ass and, well, once you go badge you never go back. Fate? Maybe so. Now, we live together as "roommates," and I have a badge of my own.

He lifted his sweaty body from my back and looked around; both of us knew the longer we kept it up, the more likely our luck would run out. As he worked himself back into his clothes, he complained, "I love you, Seth, but you have to stop speeding like this. Do I have to remind you, it's now your job to stop people like you? I won't get you out of another ticket. I mean it! Next time, not only am I going to write that ticket, no matter what interagency bullshit it stirs up between the city and state, but I'm going to do everything I can to have your license taken away if that's what it takes to keep you in one piece."

Quit speeding? I wasn't going to make him a promise I couldn't keep. And I couldn't believe he'd threatened me with handcuffs, not once, but twice! His shift would be ending in about an hour and when he got home, I'd be waiting with a horniness test of my own. Charlie would be taken down and bound with his own cuffs, begging me to make him a rookie's bitch.

THE INITIATION OF NICK VOS

Andy McGreggor

Da Vicenza was a brute of a man, an animal in a suit. But he was rich, powerful and well connected, a fact all who encountered him did well to remember. Da Vicenza had killed five times, maimed countless more and was currently where he belonged: locked up and serving ten consecutive life-sentences. Da Vicenza was lucky he had not gone to the chair, a fact he attributed to his dear lawyer, a man as venal and as corrupt as the rest of his unsavory gang of thugs. Yet Da Vicenza was not one to languish in a dank cell without his creature comforts. He was rich and he was powerful and he wished to spend his days in comfort. From the day of his arrival Da Vicenza had ruled the penitentiary with his own ruthless brand of discipline and justice. The guards were in his power. The prisoners obeyed him without question. In fact no one disobeyed Da Vicenza, not even the man's own father, who quivered in fear of his youngest son. The year was 1967, and the place was the notorious Long Reach Correctional Facility in Washington State.

Da Vicenza was fifty and weighed two hundred pounds. He worked out daily and was as strong as a bull. Women fancied him, men hated him, twinks served him if they were cute enough, but no one ignored Da Vicenza, or at least they didn't for long.

Da Vicenza was eating his lunch, a meal of higher quality than even the governor enjoyed. Da Vicenza motioned to the senior guard, a man his own age, a man as corrupt as the Devil himself.

"Who's the new boy, Brown?" asked Da Vicenza. He patted his full lips with a linen napkin.

"That is Nick Vos, Mister Da Vicenza, sir," replied the senior guard. He looked around, like the shifty weasel that he was.

"How old is he?" asked Da Vicenza, spooning crab salad into his powerful mouth. Da Vicenza's dark eyes narrowed, his handsome face creased. He dabbed a stain on his silk shirt, annoyance etched on his cruel face. "Get that cleaned," he hissed at the guard. Da Vicenza stood up and removed his shirt. Da Vicenza's body was muscular and strong. He'd taken to working out of late. The senior guard eyed Da Vicenza's body with envy. The prisoner was hairless, and as youthful as a fifty-year-old could be.

"He's nineteen, sir," replied the senior guard. "Fresh from guard training."

"I want him," said Da Vicenza tersely. He picked some crab from his teeth with his nail. "Arrange it."

"It will be done," replied the senior guard, picking up Da Vicenza's shirt. Guard or not, Brown cowered in the man's presence.

Teenage rookie Nick Vos proudly put on his uniform and looked at his trim reflection in the full-length mirror. He looked good, Vos realized proudly. The uniform hugged his body and his peaked cap highlighted his sweet, corn-fed face. Vos grinned, his white teeth flashing like pearls. Vos's eyes were like two blue sapphires, a feature he shared with his father. The Vos family was of ancient Dutch stock, and the young man's features echoed the flat landscapes of Holland. Vos brushed his blond fringe and returned his cap. He checked his stick and his cuffs. He was ready to go.

The senior guard stopped him in the corridor. He smelt of stale sweat and coffee.

"Vos," the man said. "Wait. Not so fast."

"I have to work," replied the rookie guard. He looked beyond Brown's bulk, toward the cell block.

"Yeah, and I need to fill you in," said the older man. "So shut the fuck up and listen."

"Okay," said Vos softly.

"Da Vicenza, he wants you," said the older guard, a glimmer of pity in his croaky voice.

"What do you mean?" asked Vos, his pretty face naïve and uncomprehending.

"He wants you," repeated the guard. "Do I need to spell it out?"

"No!" cried Vos. "No, that is not what I am here for. Did you tell him that is not what I am here for?" asked the young rookie guard, his forehead coated in sweat, his teen-cock hard. He'd heard the filthy rumors on induction. He'd put them down to locker-room chat.

"So come tell him yourself," muttered the guard. "Come on!"

Vos mutely followed the senior guard through the shadowy cell blocks, felons rattling the bars as they passed by. "Hey there, pretty boy!" cried a large man with a shaved head. He licked his lips salaciously as Vos walked.

"Here, son, come and suck this!" cried another man, his

impressive erection stuck through a hole in his blue uniform. "You want a filthy, pissy cock in your mouth, son?"

"Shut the fuck up," snapped Vos, hitting the bars with his stick.

"What are you gonna do about it, son? Are you gonna tell your Mommy?" taunted the man, openly masturbating.

"Go fuck yourself," replied Vos. The men laughed raucously. New guards were such fun.

They arrived at Da Vicenza's cell. In actual fact, the formidable prisoner had a suite. He had two rooms, both carpeted with Persian rugs, and instead of a metal cot, he had a single bed with a real mattress. Vos looked in amazement at the man's standard lamps, bookcases and a thick leather armchair. "Who the fuck is this guy?" whispered Vos to the senior guard.

"He's Da Vicenza," replied the senior guard, his voice hushed to a thin whisper. "You know about him."

"Where is he?" asked Vos.

"At the visitor's block," said the guard, fiddling with his clip-on tie.

"But it's not visiting day," said Vos, naïvely shocked at such a flagrant disregard of the rules.

"Shut up, sonny," replied the guard. "He's coming." They listened to the sound of approaching footsteps. Vos looked up and found himself gazing into the handsome face of Da Vicenza. The senior guard cringed. The tension was palpable. It was electric. It was dangerous.

"I brought him, sir, just as you asked, sir," the guard gushed, patches of sweat under his arms. He wiped his balding head with a handkerchief.

"Fuck off, Brown," hissed Da Vicenza. The senior guard blushed, his florid jowls turning purple. He moved away quickly. Da Vicenza eyed the young man like a hawk, his cruel brown eyes flickering. He licked his lips. "So, you are the rookie," he purred, his voice powerful, his accent a blend of New York and Salerno.

"Why aren't you in your cell, prisoner?" asked Vos, trembling. His shirt was drenched in sweat.

Da Vicenza inhaled the lad's fear and laughed a deep belly laugh. He patted the young officer on the back. "Oh, son! You *are* new, aren't you?" He pushed the young guard inside the cell. "Now you listen to me good, son," purred Da Vicenza, his fingers caressing the front of Vos's immaculate uniform. "You don't call the shots around here. I do." He smiled, flashing his white teeth. The man ripped off the lad's tie with a single swipe. Vos gasped as Da Vicenza's fingers undid the top buttons of his shirt.

"No," whispered Vos. "This is wrong," he pleaded. Da Vicenza groped the rookie's crotch, squeezing hard.

"You got a little hard-on in there, son?" teased Da Vicenza. He laughed. "Say, how about you show me that little wiener, son?"

"I am ordering you to desist," said Vos, his voice shrill, desperate to assert his authority.

Da Vicenza had the lad's zipper down and felt inside. "That's a nice little wiener, son. But it's nothing like mine. Do you wanna see my big cock, boy?" Without waiting for an answer, Da Vicenza unzipped his suit trousers. The teenage rookie looked in fascinated horror as the older man pulled out his half-hard horse cock. "That's what a man's cock looks like, son," explained Da Vicenza, pointing down at the cucumber-sized sausage.

Vos' mouth was moist, his speech slurred. "Please," he pleaded.

"Sniff that cock, boy," Da Vicenza ordered. "Get on your knees, and sniff Daddy's big, nasty fucking dick."

Vos blushed and knelt on the Persian rug. "Good boy, well done," purred Da Vicenza. He flipped off the rookie's peaked cap, and ruffled Vos's neatly combed hair. "Get that little button nose right onto that tip, boy," hissed Da Vicenza. Vos instinctively rubbed his teenage nose onto the moist tip of Da Vicenza's uncut monster cock, fifteen inches of solid, silky meat under his nostrils. The young rookie inhaled. God, the man smelt feral, thought Vos. His scent was powerful and erotic, and Vos was hooked. Vos moaned, and licked the moist, mucus-covered glans of the Mafioso's dick, strings of salty precum trailing from his pink tongue like cheese on a hot pizza.

"Not bad for a novice," said Da Vicenza, a mocking expression appearing on his face. "But this is how Daddy really likes his cock sucked," and with that the man thrust his equine cock as far as he could into Vos's throat, the lad's lovely, slim neck puffing out like a snake devouring a mouse. Vos gagged, his Sapphire eyes watering, wide with fear. Da Vicenza pushed his cock deep inside the boy's gullet and then withdrew, only to return the cucumber-sized cock afresh. With each new thrust Vos spluttered and retched, until at last he coughed up a mouthful of phlegm. His drool hung from Da Vicenza's vascular cock, like a jellyfish caught on a line. "Stand up, son," ordered Da Vicenza.

Vos stood, unsteady on his feet, wiping his mouth with the back of his hand. "Undress, boy. Take off that pretty little uniform of yours." Vos pulled off his shirt, and then peeled off his white regulation T-shirt. Vos was hairless, and his sweet body underused. Incipient love handles, barely detectable, gave his body a little padding. Da Vicenza eyed Vos's nipples sadistically. He'd have some fun with those, though maybe not today. He had some butterfly clips that would bring those boy-nips up a treat.

Vos was entranced. He trembled and he shook, but Vos craved the man's cock as a fly craves shit. *What am I doing?* he asked himself. Yet Vos was unable to control himself. He had turned into a little cocksucker with no resistance, and now he was stood, half stripped, for this lowlife criminal. "Take off your pants, boy," ordered Da Vicenza. "Tell you what, let's both take off our pants. Would you like that?" Vos nodded speechlessly. The two men stripped down to their underwear. Da Vicenza kicked Vos's utility belt under the bed.

"I'm supposed to be guarding breakfast," whispered Vos.

"Brown will cover it," said Da Vicenza. "Now, Daddy wants to look at your little wiener properly. You gonna show it to him, or do you want Daddy to pull down those little boy panties for you?" Vos stood catatonic with shame. "Did your mommy choose those little panties for you, son?" asked Da Vicenza. "Or was it your girlfriend?"

"I bought them myself," Vos said mendaciously, his voice faint.

"Sure you did," replied Da Vicenza. He yanked down the young rookie's underpants. Instinctively, Vos tried to cover his erect, six-inch cock with his hands. "Hands away," ordered Da Vicenza. He waited until Vos reluctantly complied. The lad's cock was puce, engorged, and dripping pearls of salty nectar. "Show Daddy your asshole, son," ordered Da Vicenza.

Vos stood up, and then walked to the armchair. There, he bent over to expose his plump, almost girlish buttocks. They were just perfect, thought Da Vicenza. Vos's buttocks were like two firm, white jellies, a thin dusting of golden down covering their silky surface. They were the two curtains that hid the Holy of Holies, the entrance to Vos's pristine colon. Vos shyly pulled his cheeks apart, his face in the seat of the armchair. Da Vicenza moaned softly in appreciation. There it was, he marveled, the nineteen-year-old's unplucked cherry. "That's sweet, son," said Da Vicenza hoarsely. The Mafioso took his place on the rug, like a communicant at the altar rail. Da Vicenza stuck his nose into Vos's butt and inhaled. It was a good butt, a musky, unblemished teenage butt. Da Vicenza's appetite was whetted. He licked Vos's anus until the rookie guard began to squirm and tremble. Da Vicenza roughly inserted two fingers knuckle-deep and Vos yelped.

It was good inside there, thought Da Vicenza. It was hollow and moist and hot. It was ready for a big gangster's cock. Da Vicenza would make the lad his own. He would mark his territory with his huge member. Da Vicenza sucked his fingers and nodded appreciatively at the sweet taste of the boy's clean ass. He spat on the palm of his hand, moistened his grotesquely large cock and pushed the mushroom-shaped crown of his dick into Vos's pretty anus.

"Oh god," whispered Vos. "Oh, please, sir, it burns so bad," the rookie guard whispered, tears in his eyes.

"You can take it, son," replied Da Vicenza. "Just relax. Daddy will make it feel real good soon."

"Please make it feel good," begged Vos.

Da Vicenza looked down at his handiwork. His purple, vascular cock was stuffed between the two girlish mounds of Vos's butt. "A bit more to go, son," said Da Vicenza. "Sorry. Can you stand it?"

"Yes," replied Vos. "I can take it if you want me to, sir," he replied. Da Vicenza pushed harder, and more inches of granite flesh tore past the rookie's sphincter. It hurt like a knife, and Vos winced. "Ow!" he cried softly. Vos gripped his rock-hard teen-cock and began to masturbate. Precum oozed through his fingers and formed delicate, sea-scented foam.

Finally Da Vicenza was inside his prey. Vos's pristine boy-hymen nibbled sweetly on the gangster's cock like a toothless puppy. Vos was sweating, his skin sticky and dripping. Da Vicenza began to thrust his cock in and out of the boy's butt, like a greased piston. Vos's anal lips gripped Da Vicenza's cock tightly. But Da Vicenza was close. He needed to spill his potent seed. He felt his plum-sized balls become taut and angry, fizzing and tingling in anticipation. His spine stiffened, and with a lupine roar Da Vicenza began to shoot jets of hot sperm deep into the rookie guard, coating his tissue-thin colon with the Mafioso's Satanspunk. "You fucking blond whore!" screamed Da Vicenza with a final thrust, before collapsing onto Vos's sweaty back. Panting, Da Vicenza withdrew his cock and pearls of watery, opaque cum appeared on the slit of Vos's gaping hole. Cum seeped out liberally and dripped down the lad's hairless, pink perineum. Da Vicenza wiped his softening monster cock on Vos's freshly ironed shirt, smearing spent cum and the teenage rookie's broken hymen on the blue fabric.

"Did your mommy iron that for you?" sneered Da Vicenza. Vos felt he wanted to cry but his cock was the hardest it had ever been.

"Can I cum, sir?" pleaded Vos.

"Sure son," replied Da Vicenza, with a dangerous bonhomie. "You finish yourself off." Vos wanked his six-inch cut cock, and moments later he spilled his cum into the palm of his left hand. Before Vos could react, Da Vicenza grabbed his wet hand, and forced it into Vos's shocked face. Da Vicenza rubbed the lad's palm up and down, right and left, until Vos's face was sleek with his own ejaculate.

"Don't ever, ever expect me to watch you pump your pathetic little weenie in my presence again," hissed Da Vicenza. "Do you understand?"

"Yes, sir," whimpered Vos. Vos hastily pulled on his uniform pants and buttoned his crumpled, soiled shirt. He blushed with shame and avoided Da Vicenza's strong, brown eyes.

"I expect to see you here next Tuesday, son," said Da Vicenza. "And next time, I want that little teen-cock of yours shaved, and your pussy clean for my nice big dick. You understand?"

"Yes, sir," whispered Vos, buckling his utility belt. He nervously checked that his stick, cuffs and keys were still in place.

Da Vicenza shoved an envelope into Vos's hand. "This is for you," he said evenly. "And next Tuesday, I want you to wear your boy panties a size smaller," added Da Vicenza. "So you and your mommy had better go shopping."

"Yes, sir," replied Vos, looking back over his shoulder. He walked back to his locker and hid the envelope stuffed with dollar bills. Vos was one of the guys now, as corrupt, as venal and as rotten as the rest of them.

CRIMINAL INJUSTICE

T. Hitman

Stare out a window long enough and eventually you're guaranteed to see something interesting.

For me, the long and lazy hours in that living room, that house, had passed with as much weight as the miserable orange August heat beating down from the merciless sun. My father didn't believe in air-conditioning—specifically, the cost of it. His house had bottled the heat, and the bedroom that had become my prison the previous June baked in levels too intense to endure. So I sat in the living room, which at least caught what little cross circulation of air was offered by a pair of open windows.

Still, I marinated in my sweat, aware of the sofa's itchy burnt-umber cushions, the smell of the dust baking in the vents of the television that was running nonstop to help me pass the hours as I held out diminishing hope for a preview of cool September, when the light changes, goes from direct orange to golden raining down at a cool, bent angle. September was still weeks away.

I sat and sweated, thought about enjoying one more tug, my third of the afternoon. My miserable prick of a father was a few hours from quitting time—plenty of time for me to jerk off, clean up and pray for a sudden breeze to air out the house. Problem was, my life had degenerated to masturbation as the highlight of the day, with thoughts about writing in between. The writing had become masturbation after a fashion, too; my laptop hummed, its battery depleted down below half, though my fingers had only fucked around on a lone sentence displayed on an otherwise white screen. I dabbled longhand but gave up when the sweat from below my wrist stuck my skin to the page and made the empty blue lines bleed.

I was lost and hot and itchy and bored.

And then I glanced out the window, alerted to a flicker of movement in the orange afternoon haze, and saw him. The heat in the house doubled. Part of me died; something deep within my wilted soul was reborn.

"Fuck," I sighed, and wondered if I'd snapped, or was suffering the effect of a heat stroke.

I blinked. The vision remained, moved closer on huge bare feet. The man stood, I guessed, somewhere past the six-foot mark, six-two, maybe six-three. His chest was bare like his feet; my eyes fell into the gravitational pull exerted by muscles solid without being showy, a defined six-pack abdomen. The T-pattern of hair superimposed over it all cutting down the middle took a brief detour around his naval before plunging beneath the top of faded blue jeans, his only stitch of clothing. A rip over one knee flashed leg muscles, equally magnificent and furry. Those big feet begged to be worshiped.

Forcing my eyes back up took extra effort. His dark hair was military neat, not a single strand out of place. A shadow of five o'clock scruff coated his handsome face at four in the afternoon. Even from the distance between living room window, across driveway and a patch of lawn to the pockmarked surface of Juniper Road, I could tell that the young man's eyes were beyond blue. Sapphire gemstones gazed up, connecting to mine. The cool relief I'd craved briefly rolled over me in a shiver. Heat followed in its wake, mercilessly unpleasant. I choked down a heavy swallow to find my mouth completely dry.

He saw me staring out. And right when I thought I couldn't take it for another second, the hot young man moseying down the road with his hands tucked in his front pockets flashed me a smile.

I suddenly found my pen fueled with high-octane ink. My fingers flew across the page and keyboard. Several poems, a short story and the second chapter of a stalled novel rose from inertia by the weekend's conclusion. Muse, yes—but the handsome dude also inspired fiercer masturbation. Between the hours of work in the oven of my bedroom, I beat my dick to thoughts of a man who seemed to fall to Earth from the sun.

My name is Gunner. At the end of my freshmen year at a liberal arts college in Vermont, I moved back to my father's place. Here was never home, and apart from providing the roof over my head, which he reminded me of constantly, he was never much of a dad. For most of the summer, I'd locked myself in the bedroom he set up for weekend visits following the divorce, except when the heat grew unbearable and he left for work.

That weekend, not even his sour mood affected my excitement, for I'd crossed paths with a demigod.

With the first real smile on my face since returning to the town of Salem, I walked out the front door and followed the dude's course in reverse, hoping there would be a second coming. A bloated red sun floated above the pines. Heat baked the world.

Juniper turned onto Dean Avenue, an older development of single-story ranches, a garrison on the corner and, at the far end of the road, a trio of garden-style rental units, two levels each, pushed back against seventy acres of dense woods you just knew wouldn't survive for long once the housing market rebounded.

An old Stevie Wonder tune about not worrying 'bout a thing drifted through my head. I walked in no particular hurry, a dreamy grin tempting my expression. Hands tucked into my pockets, mirroring his moves, I tried to ignore the weight of my balls, which hung like lead ingots beneath the fullness of my dick, pinned half-erect at an awkward angle. In T-shirt and sneakers, jeans, a stylish black fedora I'd picked up at a used-clothing store near the campus in Vermont, I felt good again, almost whole. The midlife crisis that had latched on to me twenty years early relaxed its grip. I drew in a deep breath. The air smelled of lawns and pine sap and old asphalt cooking in the August sun, the mixture nearly narcotic in its potency.

In a daze, I reached the circular drive leading around the front entrances of the Dean Gardens. Thoughts of the handsome demigod threatened to pump my cock up to its full hardness. I turned the fingers of my right hand inward, brushed its shaft and saw stars as well as the sun. Too much more and I risked making an obvious wet mess at the front of my jeans.

I started to circle the Dean Gardens driveway, wondered if he was one of the tenants recently moved in during the summer or my absence at college. School. Should I go back? I sure as fuck wasn't staying in my father's place. I'd land a job, any job, finish getting my MFA even if the route was circuitous, the long way around. Like the driveway at Dean Gardens.

"What the fuck are you looking at?" a deep male voice demanded, drawing me out of imaginary clouds.

I blinked. A gazebo rose at the center of an island of sunburned grass and tufts of hearty weeds. I glanced up to see a figure leaning against one of the posts, the source of that angry dog growl. It wasn't the handsome young demigod, but a demon in a leather jacket and jeans and shit-kicker boots, with a decent amount of ink displayed on his throat. My eyes fell into the fungus-colored patterns superimposed over his Adam's apple. A burst of orange, just higher, broke the spell. The demon sucked on a cigarette and exhaled a brimstone breath. Attractive in a brutish way, yes, but clearly trouble. The kind of man you didn't fuck with. Besides, I wasn't here to see him.

"You talking to me?" I asked, clearly channeling De Niro in that hat.

"Yeah, you, dick-licker. What business you got here?"

"No business."

"Then I suggest you turn your faggot ass around and beat feet as far away and as fast as your legs can carry you."

I stood frozen for a long second or so, stunned by what he said. I was no slouch; if beating off can be considered a form of exercise, on that count I had the body of a dude who lived at the gym. Still, I sensed it was smarter to bow out of this particular fight before it began.

"Whatev," I chuckled, and started back in the direction of my father's house, that prison.

A low thrum cut through the humidity. I tipped my gaze in the direction of Juniper Road, saw a black pickup truck motoring in from the far end of Dean, and glanced back, toward the gazebo. Tats was gone. I tracked the dude's last exhale of cancer smoke toward a corner of the rightmost building. The door to an apartment on the second floor slammed into place. A curtain stirred. I could tell I was being watched and resumed walking, intending to write off the afternoon as a bust.

The pickup pulled beside me. I stared through the open passenger's window at the driver, forgot about the creep with the cigarette and tatted throat, along with the knowledge that I—we—were being watched from one of the apartments. I almost forgot my own name.

One hand on the wheel, the handsomest man in the history of the human race leaned toward me. He thumbed up the bill of his policeman's hat with the other and flashed a smile that threatened to dissolve my insides. Dark hair. Eyes beyond simple blue—sapphire gemstones. A dimple blossomed on one cheek through a thin coat of late-day scruff. Police uniform. The demigod from that other afternoon offered a tip of his chin.

"'Sup, dude?"

I opened my mouth, intending to speak, but at first no words emerged. "Not much," I eventually managed.

Our eyes connected fully. I fell into the hypnotic pull of his gaze, and my flesh ignited. My cock thickened. Breathing suddenly wasn't so easy or involuntary.

"I saw you, the other day," he said.

"Yeah, I saw you," I answered.

"Name's Steve. Steve Ranley."

I committed his name to memory, knowing I'd howl it later into my pillow as I jerked myself in the muggy darkness. Not sure why, I told him my name and fired off a salute. "Pleased to meet you, Officer."

Steve Ranley's smile widened. "Cut that shit, Gunner—I've only worn this badge for three weeks."

"Yes, Sir."

He narrowed his eyes. "Dude, you want to hang out? Watch the game?"

"What game?'

"The baseball game, fool."

"You and me?"

"Sure. I'm new to town, don't know a lot of people. Building three, apartment four—the one on the bottom right."

Steve aimed his chin at the same building where the dick with the ink and attitude had retreated. The rookie cop's place was directly beneath that apartment. I broke focus with his magnificence long enough to face building three, and I was sure we were still being watched, if the sensation slithering over my flesh was to be trusted.

"Can I bring anything?" I asked.

"Just your ass, pal. Give me an hour to get human."

I blinked myself out of the spell, ignored the strange premonition that something in that other apartment above Steve Ranley's wasn't right and then returned all of my attention to the demigod. "See you in sixty."

Our eyes lingered. In that bottled gaze, I absorbed the radiance of his smile, the piney scent of his skin among the truck exhaust and the lush green smell of the surrounding planet, and did my best to ignore the itchy weight of my dick, puffed up to its thickest as a result of my second meeting with a man so handsome it hurt to face him directly for too long, like staring at the summer sun.

A hand hammered on the bathroom door.

"Yeah," I called.

"How long you gonna be in there?" my father barked.

I rolled my eyes. "Just a sec."

The sec was more like five minutes, time enough to rub one out over thoughts of the handsome rookie cop, my new friend. I bit back a bellow and squirted my load down the drain, hoping the release would keep my dick satisfied—and soft—when I stood again in his presence. Conflicted as to whether I should even go and worrying about the risk of being found out—worse, unsure whether the chemical explosion I felt for Steve Ranley connected only in one direction, not two—I dried off, buttoned my jeans and exited the head, only to fall under my father's ugly scrutiny.

"Where you going?" I grumbled.

"Out."

"Out where?"

Socks and T-shirt in hand, I started toward my bedroom, where the closed door trapped the day's heat, turning my prison volcanic.

"Wait."

I dug in my soles. "Just to a friend's," I said over my shoulder. "To watch the baseball game."

"Oh, now you're suddenly into sports?" He exhaled through his nostrils, and I didn't need to turn around to gauge the sour look on his face. "How's that job hunt going?"

I continued through the door, into Hell.

Before the door closed, I heard him mutter, "Real good, that's what I thought."

I sat on my bed and sweated. My stomach grumbled, knotted after suffering numerous invisible punches. At that moment, my lowest of the summer, I forgot all about Steve Ranley and our strange, new relationship. My attention settled on my backpack. The urge to shove my laptop and some clothes into it, to walk out the door and keep on walking, tempted me.

An unexpected breeze swept into the room, cooling my anger. Instead, I walked out of my father's house and turned down Dean Avenue for my night with the rookie cop.

The scent of green spaces, mowed lawns and summer embraced me. I retraced my steps to the trio of garden-style apartments. No angry sphinx guarded the gazebo this time. My heart attempted to jump into my throat on the final approach to the building. A curtain was drawn over the glass slider to the right of Steve's front door. I realized it was a bedsheet, a makeshift solution for a guy newly arrived to life in an unfamiliar town.

Making a fist stilled my shaking fingers. I knocked. Breathless seconds later, Steve answered the door.

"Dude," he greeted me through a cocksure grin.

In a short time, I quietly recorded his details: harvest-yellow tank top, same blue jeans from our first encounter, the rip showing hairy leg muscles, big bare feet. I tried to not stare— or feel insignificant in the company of a man so magnificent. Reminding myself that Steve wanted me there helped.

"Come on in. Mind the mess," he said.

The mess was contained within two small rooms separated by a tiny kitchen and what I assumed was the bathroom, to the right behind a closed door. The living room seemed comprised of hand-me-down furniture, what there was of it. Only the flat-screen TV was new.

The baseball pregame played on mute. I noticed Steve's police uniform on a hanger, hooked onto the top of the ajar bedroom door, his big shiny boots propped in front, an impromptu jamb.

It was a dude's place, and I felt instantly consumed by curiosity because of the young man who lived there.

"Nice," I sighed.

"It does okay for now."

He closed the door, strutted into the kitchen and grabbed a pair of longnecks from the fridge. Steve handed one over, his eyes drinking in my details, too. He raised his bottle.

"To new friends," he said.

"Cheers."

We toasted.

* * *

Pizza arrived. Before I could tell Steve I didn't have any green on me, he paid with a twenty. I gulped down the rush of embarrassment at feeling inferior. Two boxes—pepperoni in one, double cheese in the other.

"So," he said, eyeing me while chomping on his second slice. "What's your story?"

The choice of words made me smile. "Funny you should put it so."

I told him about my crazy dream of being a writer; my escape from college; my father.

"I want to read your stuff," Steve said.

My smile widened. "And you?"

Oldest of two sons, parents divorced like mine, he grew up a few towns away. Steve had graduated the police academy near the top of his class, and was presently taking criminal justice courses at the local college. He wanted to make detective, but for now was paying his dues. "Aren't we all," he said, then, "Girlfriend?"

A shiver raced through me. I answered with a shake of my head. "You?"

"Used to, but the distance, you know, and..."

"And?"

"Girls aren't really my thing anymore. I'm into..."

The air clotted around me. My heart hammered a drum solo into my ears. I gulped down the last of my beer. The rush of suds left me light-headed. I sputtered, rose. Suddenly, Steve was there, right in front of me, blocking escape, his bright eyes capturing mine.

"You," he said. "I'm into you, dude."

The world phased out of focus. Steve leaned closer, and our mouths crushed together. I thought I'd pass out from the surge of energy, light and fire. The empty beer bottle slipped from my hand. My first instinct was to pull away. The last sane sliver inside my skull said no, no—and I kissed back. Steve reached up, seized the back of my neck and pinned me against him with the other hand clamped against the small of my spine. A supernova that only I could see erupted before my eyes after our groins collided. Cocks ground, both hard.

"Yes," I mouthed around his kisses.

Steve backed me toward the small bedroom. His police uniform appeared in the space above my eyes as the glare of exploding stars died down enough to see again. Steve wanted me. There was no longer any question. The handsome young cop was mine.

He groaned something untranslatable in words but easy to understand through action. I slipped my butt onto the edge of the mattress, reached toward the bottom of his yellow tank. Steve broke our lip-lock, yanked the shirt over his head and bared that amazing chest. I caught the warm scent of his skin, the masculine smell of his deodorant, and reached up, steadying my hand on his chest muscles. Then my fingers walked down, down, at long last reaching the top of his jeans. I unbuttoned, unzipped. Steve's jeans dropped.

In the last of the daylight filtering in through the sparse gaps in the sheet-curtain and the dense network of trees outside, I made out of the details of Steve's body, especially the formfitting pair of dark red boxer-briefs spray-painted onto his crotch and thighs. His legs were more incredible close up, in the flesh, than in any of my jerk-off fantasies. He stepped out of his jeans. Steve's feet, too, were the stuff of dreams.

His dick stood stiffly at the front of his underwear, inviting my touch. Permission already granted in groans, I reached up, squeezed. A glop of wetness spilled under my fingers. Steve moaned and pushed against me.

"Oh fuck," he huffed, his voice barely above a whisper. "That's right, buddy. Do it. Yeah…"

I hooked my fingers into the elastic waistband of his boxer-briefs and pulled. His shorts followed his jeans. Steve's cock bounced up, its length perfect, its girth ideal. Two bloated nuts hung heavy beneath, their fragrance filling my next shallow sip of air. A nest of dark curls wreathed all.

Licking my lips, I moved closer. His cock entered my mouth. Nothing before, none of my few flirtations and experimentations at college, had prepared me for the awesomeness of Steve Ranley. The pulsing, rubbery thickness on my tongue satisfied me fully, body, mind and soul. I fondled Steve's balls, breathed in his male scent, sucked. The musky tang of his precome ignited on my taste buds. I managed to take most of him, gagged, but put to practice everything I'd learned watching men give head to other men on the Internet.

Steve grunted his approval. I glanced up to see him smiling, his eyes half-closed, and smiled, too.

"Play with my nuts some more," he commanded.

I gave them a series of tugs and tickles, worked my thumb behind them and caressed the sensitive patch of skin between his bag and asshole.

"Keep that up and I'm gonna bust!"

I hadn't forgotten my own needs, but at Steve's declaration, I could only focus on his. I sucked harder, faster, and did my best to get that last neglected inch or so of cock into my mouth. His curls teased my nostrils.

Uncounted plunges later, Steve kept good on his word and unloaded his seed across my tongue. I swallowed him down, and then he pulled free, dumping the last of his nectar on my face and then, lowering to lick it off my mouth without hesitation. Our lips again connected, and we kissed.

* * *

Saying nothing, Steve stripped me. I was his, and I put my trust completely in him. Sneakers and socks, shirt and jeans. My underwear went last into a pile on the floor. My complaining cock aimed its head upward, anxious at the promise of what was soon to follow.

"Sweet," Steve said.

I noticed his dick, recently spent, had lost none of its stiffness. He shot a mischievous glance through narrowed eyes at me, bent for a taste and the world again erupted in blinding spindles of light.

"Holy shit," I cried.

The holy element in the statement deepened when, during our localized repeat performance of the Big Bang that first gave birth to the cosmos, his tongue moved behind my balls, and Steve claimed my asshole through a succession of hungry, wet licks.

Two condoms congealed on the nightstand, each filled with Steve's wad. My head rested in the sweaty protection of his armpit. I caressed his cock, again up and dripping with semen.

Steve kissed the top of my head. "Fuck, that was great."

Our mouths briefly reconnected, long enough for him to taste his skeet on my breath and for me to recognize my asshole on his lips.

My eyes settled on the dark space of the ceiling. "Can I ask you something? The dude that lives up there..."

"Two dudes, I think. What about them?"

"Two?" I relived the strange encounter, the sense of being watched. "You think there's something suspicious going on up there?"

Steve shrugged. "What do you mean? That they're having fun, like us down here?"

He reached lower and smacked my ass.

I considered sucking on his cock, only the word was past my lips before I could censor it. "Something criminal. Earlier today..."

I shared the story.

"Maybe it's just my writer's imagination working overtime, but the one with the throat tats...it's like he was on the lookout, keeping tabs on you, your comings and goings."

Steve drew in a hit of breath. "Maybe. Speaking of coming..."

"I'm serious."

"So am I."

Sometime past three in the morning, I slid out of Steve's bed and began to pull on clothes in the darkness.

Steve exhaled a tired sigh. "Why don't you stay, dude?"

"My old man will be seriously pissed if I'm out all night." I stuffed socks into pockets, pulled sneakers onto bare feet. "Thanks. I had a great night. The fucking best."

"Let's do it again."

"Deal," I said, and pecked Steve on the cheek.

He grabbed my arm as I rose to leave, reeled me back to him, and kissed me fully on the lips. "Tonight. I insist."

I nodded and caressed his cheek, now showing decent stubble in the shadows. I didn't fully recognize the emotion that filled me, but considered that it might be love. Two men had met and fallen into bed. Was it possible they'd also fallen for something deeper?

"Goodnight, handsome," I said.

I navigated Steve's apartment, exited through the front door and walked out into a warm, wondrous night lit by the glow of the streetlights. I licked my lips, again tasted Steve, and found myself willing to believe. I wanted to skip, my plodding steps freed of the weight of the summer's previous gravitational misery.

An instant after I caught the acrid stink of cigarette smoke, a hand clamped over my mouth. Another grabbed hold of my shirt collar, dragging me off the pavement and toward the darkness behind the apartment building.

"Don't you fucking cry out," a man's voice hissed at my ear.

Something cold and brutally sharp poked at the flesh near my right kidney. I froze. A spark lit in the darkness among the pines—a lighter's flame. A red ember glowed before me. The dude with the inked throat sucked a hit and then exhaled the noxious breath into my face. I wanted to sputter, but fear of being cut by the blade made me suffer the insult in silence.

"Good," Tats said. "Let me tell you how this works: we ask the questions, and you answer. If you don't, Jerry here's gonna stick you."

The Blade delivered a poke just painful enough to telegraph the very serious danger I now faced.

"You understand?" asked the voice at my back.

I nodded.

"Your butt-fuck buddy in there, the cop who moved into this shit-hole. What does he know?"

"Know?" I parroted. "About what?"

The Blade jabbed me, and excruciating pain flared across my flesh in concentric circles. I knew he'd pierced my skin. I bit back a shriek as the night turned an angry shade of crimson before my eyes.

"I swear," I started.

"Upstairs, in the apartment above his. How much does he know?"

"He doesn't," I said, blinking rapidly in an attempt to clear the filter of red. "He's a rookie, new to town."

"What were you doing in there all night?" This, from Tats.

"Sucking his dick, just like you accused me of earlier this afternoon. He doesn't suspect anything at all. Hell, I won't tell him," I lied. "I'll make sure my mouth is too full of dick to utter a single word."

"Fucking homo," Tats huffed.

Then he nailed me with a hard sucker punch to the guts. All the air fled my lungs. The red haze evaporated in a rush of black dots. I dropped to my knees, the few feet seeming more like the distance of falling into a bottomless pit.

Facing what could well be my death, the injustice of it all hit home fully. After the unhappy summer in my father's house and the lowest time of my young life, I'd met a handsome policeman who not only made me feel great about myself, but wanted to know me better, to be with me. Lying in Steve's bed postcoitus, I'd imagined the potential beyond our first night together. There'd be a second, for sure. And I had decided to enroll in the local community college and work toward my MFA, find work as a freelance writer in the meanwhile. I'd escape my father's humorless house—maybe Steve would ulti- mately ask me to move in with him. I'd be happy. I was— fucking joyous, in fact, for the first time in a long string of days. Only now two criminal dickheads had me on the ground, gasping for breath.

No, I wasn't giving up all I saw in my future. I willed my lungs to fill with air and, as the two criminals snickered above me, I focused on their voices, tracked them in the darkness.

I threw all of the strength left in me into punches and nailed them both in the junk.

I ran blindly toward what I thought was the direction of the

building. Pine branches clawed at my face. Footfalls and malev-
olent voices sounded behind me.

"Steve," I called out. "Steve!"

I stumbled, fell, picked myself up and resumed running.
The night broke in the wan glow of streetlights. I rounded the
building, and there he stood, my Steve, dressed only in those
formfitting red boxer-briefs.

My hero.

He pulled me into his arms, and then guided me protectively
behind his musculature as Blade and Tats caught up.

The rest after that eventually became fodder for my pen, and
the stuff of legend.

HOMECOMING

Michael Bracken

Keeping my two lives separate is tearing me apart. I'm a narcotics officer, and for several weeks or even for several months at a time I work undercover, unable to contact my life partner. When I do have the chance to return home, it is often without notice, surprising Joshua with my sudden appearance in our bedroom. He welcomes me each time, but I sense a growing distance between us, one that may become too great to overcome if the current investigation doesn't soon reach a conclusion, and I fear he will turn to another for the things I'm rarely there to provide.

We met when I was a rookie, just out of the academy and doing ride-alongs with an experienced officer. On my second day we were called to the scene of an assault—a mugging that had turned violent when Joshua refused to relinquish his wallet to a pair of street punks. He was sitting on the curb when we arrived, a bruise on his cheek already darkening, a young woman from a nearby salon sitting next to him. She had called in the assault while it was still in progress, but we had arrived too late to stop it.

Joshua gave us a lopsided grin and said, "They didn't get anything."

We did our job—taking statements, filling out paperwork, and so on—but I saw the way my training officer treated Joshua as if he were a suspect and not a victim, and I knew I would need to keep my sexual orientation a closely guarded secret if I hoped to advance within the department.

I don't know why, but I stopped at Joshua's apartment after I clocked out that night. My excuse was that he had refused medical attention at the scene and I worried that had made too hasty a decision. When he opened the door, I saw that the bruise on his cheek had darkened, but he appeared no worse for his encounter with the punks who'd tried to take his wallet.

I was out of uniform so it took him a moment to realize who I was. When he did, he stiffened. "Yes, Officer Kirk?"

"Terry. Call me Terry," I said. "I wanted to assure myself that you were okay."

"Is this part of the department's new community outreach?"

"No," I said. I told him I was two days on the force and, until called to the scene of his assault, had been involved with nothing more complicated than moving violations.

"Is that any reason to treat me the way you did?"

"No," I said. "My partner—"

"Don't blame your partner," he said. "You're responsible for your own actions."

He was correct, and I've carried that message with me throughout my career. "I apologize."

Joshua looked me up and down. "You want to come in? I'll fix us something to drink."

I hadn't thought that far ahead when I'd parked in front of

his apartment building, but soon I sat on his couch, a Jack-and-Coke in my fist. Joshua sat on the other end of the couch.

Despite the bruise, he was an attractive young man, with finger-length blond hair, soft but symmetrical features, and sparkling blue eyes. He sipped his drink and eyed me over the top of his glass. After he swallowed, he said, "You didn't come here just out of the goodness of your heart."

I remained silent.

"You want me, don't you? I see it in your eyes. I saw it in your eyes this afternoon, but you were fighting your feelings then. Now...now you're not."

Joshua knew what I wanted without my asking. After setting his glass on the end table, he closed the distance between us. He placed one hand on my thigh and reached up with the other to brush the backs of his fingers along my jawline.

I tensed, unsure what would happen next. My cock knew. It twitched and battled with the entangling folds of my boxer shorts as it began to swell and tent my pants. I downed the last of my Jack-and-Coke and set my glass aside.

"Kiss me," Joshua whispered, his face only inches from mine. "You know you want to."

I had not been with a man since before entering the academy, and I'd been careful while there not to reveal my carnal desires, but now I had no reason to hold back. I captured his head between my hands, careful of his bruise, and covered his lips with mine. We kissed hard and deep and long, our teeth clicking together, our tongues entwining.

As we kissed, our fingers fumbled with buttons and buckles and zippers and shoelaces, stripping away our clothes and strewing things around the living room. Soon we were naked and Joshua knelt on the living room floor between my wide-spread legs as I sat on the couch. My cock stood at attention mere inches from Joshua's face, and his warm breath tickled it each time he exhaled.

He wrapped one fist around the base of my stiff shaft and glanced up at me. Then he wrapped his lips around the spongy soft helmet head of my cock, hooking his teeth behind the glans, and painted my cockhead with his tongue.

As he tongued my cock, Joshua began moving his fist up and down the length of my shaft, and each time his hand slid to the base of my cock, he took a little more into his mouth. When he had engulfed more than half of my cock, he drew back until only my cockhead remained. Then he did it again and again.

A bit of precum escaped from the tip of my cock. He sucked me clean. My cock grew harder, my balls tightened, and it was obvious to both of us that I was about to come when I began thrusting my hips upward to meet his descending mouth.

He grabbed my ball sac with his free hand and squeezed.

And then I came, firing hot spunk against the back of Joshua's throat. He swallowed every drop before he drew his face away.

He smiled, stood and took my hand. "Let's take this to the bedroom."

His erect cock led the way. Once there he reached into the drawer of his nightstand and pulled out an unopened tube of lube. He opened the tube, squeezed a glob into his hand and covered my limp cock with it. I began to regain my former stature, so I took the lube from Joshua and made him turn around.

As he bent over and leaned against the wall, I slathered lube into his asscrack, massaged it into his tight sphincter until it loosened enough I could slip a finger into him. Then I stepped behind him and replaced my finger with the head of my cock, pressing forward. His sphincter resisted at first, but there was so much lube slathered on my shaft and in his hole that it didn't take much effort to bury my cock inside him.

I drew back and pressed forward as he braced himself against the wall. My right hand was covered with lube, so I reached around and wrapped my fist around his erect cock. It was a little awkward to jerk him off while I was driving into him from behind, but I managed.

He came first, firing a thin stream of spunk against the bedroom wall, and then I came, emptying my second load inside him.

We leaned against the wall for a moment while my throbbing cock slowly softened and finally slipped out of his ass. Then we collapsed across his bed.

We never did find the punks who had assaulted Joshua, but if it hadn't been for them we might never have met, and our relationship never would have developed from that first meeting into something permanent.

For several years, until the department's attitude loosened up, we maintained separate residences. Then, less then a year before I was sent undercover, we purchased a house together—a house I visited far too infrequently.

Inside I'm still the rookie cop Joshua fell in love with; outside I'm anything but. I'd been clean-cut in those days. I'm not now, with greasy, shoulder-length hair, a scraggly beard, and tattoos I never would have gotten if I hadn't needed them to enhance my undercover persona. Each time I return home Joshua comments on the changes in my appearance, and each time I assure him that they are only temporary.

Three months have passed since I've last been home. My hair has grown even longer, and I've gained a tattoo. I'm remembering our first time together as I push my way into our bedroom, led by an erection that quickly deflates when I see two shapes beneath the covers. Much as I'd feared, Joshua has taken another lover in my absence.

I switch on the overhead light, surprising both occupants of the bed. Joshua sits up, but his bed partner leaps at me, teeth bared, hackles raised, a growl erupting from his throat, and I back away.

Joshua calls the dog, wraps a fist in the black lab's collar and assures me I'm safe from Rookie.

I laugh long and hard, collapsing on the bed with my life partner and his new companion. When I catch my breath I tell him of my fear.

"You're right," Joshua explains. "I need company, but no man can replace you. Even so, I need someone I can love who will love me and make me feel safe while you're away. And Rookie does that."

I decide right then to request a transfer back to plainclothes and regular hours as soon as my current assignment ends. Then I scratch Rookie's head and gather Joshua in my arms.

My welcome-home kiss is everything I had hoped for.

OPEN-MINDED

D. K. Jernigan

You ready for some action, Rookie?" Tony Stein pulled their squad car to the curb in front of a building. The lot was commercial, or had been at one point, but it looked mostly abandoned, with only some faded signs announcing JASMINE'S MASSAGE in one dark window showing any signs of life.

Chris, who was already getting more than sick of being called Rookie, gave the building a critical once-over. "What, squatters?"

"Better," Tony answered, a grin spreading across his face like a stain. "Prostitutes."

Chris turned to study the building again. Perhaps it was not so much abandoned or decrepit as it was camouflaged—carefully not whitewashed or prettied up so that it wouldn't get passing attention. But there were a couple of cars on the far side of the lot in front of a boarded-up fast-food place. The hookers?

Tony was already out of the car, and Chris hurried to back him up. Not that Tony acted like he needed any backup. Chris was mostly left to admire the tight curves of Tony's ass as the experienced cop strode straight to the door, knocked twice and pushed it open. Chris flinched at the total lack of procedure, and clenched his fists, which were dying to twitch for his gun or his radio like they were safety blankets.

Inside, a small, dark-haired woman smiled broadly, her eyes crinkling at the corners the only giveaway that she was not as young as she appeared. She stood up and crossed the room in two long strides, taking Tony's hand and kissing his cheek. "You look so tired today! Are you stressed? You should relax. Eva is working tonight; she would love to see to you..." Her voice was softly accented and dark and it made Chris shiver even though he'd never looked at a woman that way in his life.

He waited for Tony to cuff her, but he only started chatting. "Aren't we going to arrest her?" he asked, incredulous.

"Arrest her? For what?"

"For...solicitation." Chris felt like he had walked onto the set of a game show, and he didn't know the rules.

Tony, however, knew them by heart. He burst out laughing, and Chris felt his face flame. "Damn, rookie, cool off a little bit. Mirela will make sure that you get taken care of, too."

"I haven't—I'm not—" Since it had already been red, his face must have looked like a beacon by now.

Two busty young things wandered into the room, and Tony gestured to them with a negligent wave. "Come on, Rookie, you telling me that doesn't warm your blood up, some? Just relax a little bit; this was supposed to be your welcoming surprise, huh?"

"I'm just not—" What the fuck was he supposed to say? Chris took a step back and turned, distancing himself from the whole scene. Tony swore softly behind him.

"Mirela, babe, can we get a room?"

"Second to your left. Just throw the girls out," the madam said.

Tony jerked his head, and Chris followed, humiliation and frustration fighting for dominance inside him. A welcoming surprise? What the fuck was that supposed to mean?

The two women chatting in the small room left easily at Tony's request, and he shut the door behind them before turning to face Chris, who had stepped two steps past him into the room.

"There's an arrangement around here. These lovely ladies enjoy their small business, while not hurting anyone, and as long as we all keep things polite, the local cops can stop in for a 'massage' from time to time. Okay?"

"Fine, but I'm just not—I can wait in the car for you. No big deal." Chris started toward the door, but Tony stepped in front of him.

"They're clean and careful. What's your problem? No wife... girlfriend?" Chris shook his head. "Then what? You'd have to be a fag not to spring one around those girls," Tony scoffed. But he'd caught Chris's flinch when he used the word "fag." "Are you? You gay, Rookie?"

"No, I'm not," Chris said, but he couldn't meet Tony's eyes. How the fuck had this come out so soon? He'd been hoping to be well established on the force before anyone ever caught on, by which point he could blow it off as no big deal. Hey, I'm one of the guys, right? I ever made a pass at any of you? Okay, then...

But it was looking much too late to hope for that. "You are, aren't you, Rookie? You take it up the ass? You like big, strong men instead of those dainty flowers out there?"

"Look, can we just go? I'm just not into hookers, okay?"

"So who you into, Rookie?"

Chris stared at the wall over Tony's shoulder and kept his mouth shut. What the hell do you say to something like that?

"You know, I fancy myself an open-minded man," Tony continued. "I was planning to get my rocks off tonight, and there ain't no sense in you missing out on the fun, now is there?" Tony hitched up his service belt and waggled his brows at Chris, who would have blushed if he had any blood left to blush with—it had all raced south, and his cock stretched his pants into a horrifying tent. Tony saw it and smirked. "What do you say, Rookie? You gonna get my rocks off tonight?"

Chris's eyes were wide and his mouth was dry as he stared at his partner. Open-minded? Was he *serious*? His cock throbbed painfully, and a small sound of arousal escaped before he could contain it.

Tony grinned, and locked the door. "I've always had this secret fantasy," he said, advancing on the frozen Chris, "of having my way with some prisoner, sometime. I'd never do it," he clarified, "but that don't mean I don't jerk to it if the mood hits me right."

He reached for the buckle of Chris's belt, and Chris felt helpless to resist. It took only moments for Tony to strip him down to his undershirt and boxers, and Chris could already feel a damp patch where precome was soaking the shorts. He panted, and his cock twitched restlessly, desperate. It was like some fucking fantasy, only about a thousand times better, and featuring the gorgeous new partner he'd only just begun to dream about.

He actually moaned when Tony reached behind his back and came up with his cuffs. One of the cold bracelets snapped around Chris's wrist, and Tony locked the cuff and twisted his arm behind his back to complete the "arrest."

"Now on your knees, scumbag," Tony said, a smirk still tickling at the edge of his mouth. Chris wanted to kiss that smirk away, but he sank slowly to his knees. The carpet was plush enough to be comfortable—probably not a coincidence. As Tony unzipped his fly, Chris mused that plenty of people probably spent hours on their knees in this room and rooms like it.

But then Tony's cock was in his face, long and still slowly thickening with arousal, and he couldn't think of anything but how mouthwateringly beautiful it looked.

"You want this?" Tony asked, wagging his cock in Chris's face. He swung it so that it slapped against one of Chris's cheeks, then the other. "Huh? You want my cock, scumbag? Doesn't matter, because you're going to take it anyway, aren't you?"

"Yes," Chris breathed. His eyes were locked on Tony's erection, now almost completely full, and longer than any he'd taken before. He licked his lips eagerly, and Tony grunted in satisfaction.

"That's 'Yes, Officer Stein,' you punk."

"Yes, Officer Stein," he repeated dutifully. Tony grabbed him by the hair and yanked his head back. When Chris opened his mouth to yelp, he found Tony's cock being shoved down his throat. Tony was neither gentle nor patient. His cock rammed in deep, and Chris gagged and choked as the thick flesh speared his throat. He fought desperately against the urge to throw up, and found distraction in the sensations of his own cock. Tony was thrusting so hard that Chris's whole body rocked with the motion, and his cock rubbed gently against the inside of his boxers, teasing and tantalizing the nerves that were already desperately sensitive.

He focused on the way his cock felt as it dragged over the soft fabric, and found it easier to match Tony's rhythm with his throat, swallowing the length of him as Tony skull-fucked him. It took him by surprise when the pleasure in his cock mounted and his balls drew up, and the next thing he knew, he was convulsing helplessly in Tony's grasp and moaning around Tony's cock, his entire body tense with release as his hot come coated the inside of his boxers.

Tony pushed away, and Chris gasped a grateful breath as the pleasure continued to wash through him, only magnified by the humiliation of creaming his shorts.

"You really are a pervert, aren't you, Rookie?" Tony asked. His smirk had only grown, and Chris felt helplessly aroused by the sight of it, and of Tony wrapping one thick hand around his equally thick cock and stroking slowly—thoughtfully.

"I think I like this open-minded shit. Okay, Prisoner Rookie, on your feet. I think you liked that way too much. We're going to have to get creative, now." Tony helped pull Chris to his feet and then guided him to the small bed against the back wall of the room. "Bend over and spread 'em, scumbag, we're gonna do a strip search."

He yanked Chris's boxers off and threw them across the room with a disgusted look. "I don't have any rubber gloves on me, today," he said, the smirk being joined by a twinkle in his eye, "so I guess we're going to have to use something else." He tore a condom package open, and Chris felt his cock pulse slightly. Holy shit, already?

Tony rolled the condom on, humming to himself as he did it. "Spread 'em nice and wide, scumbag. We've got to be real sure you don't have any contraband between those sweet cheeks." His big cock probed at the entry to Chris's hole, and Chris moaned and pushed back, helping Tony past those tight muscles. He nearly sobbed with pleasure as he felt Tony slide home, deep inside his passage. The thick, long cock stretched and teased him, and he squeezed, making Tony hiss.

"You think you're funny, scumbag?"

"No, sir. Officer Stein."

Tony thrust, starting with a steady rhythm that made Chris desperate for an earth-shattering pounding. He pushed back against each thrust and squeezed his muscles around Tony's cock, urging and tantalizing with his body. He hissed when Tony grabbed the chain between his cuffs, forcing the cool metal to bite into his wrists, but Tony used the leverage to increase his pace, and Chris wasn't complaining.

"Too good for you," Tony hissed, and his pace slowed a little. Something clanked on his belt, and then Tony's nightstick appeared in front of Chris's face. Tony held it with both hands and forced it between Chris's teeth. When he increased his pace again, Chris bit down to keep it in place and howled in pleasure. His ass was being split and filled by the most gorgeous cock he'd laid eyes on in ages, and he was being used for his hot partner's pleasure. His cock took another jump, climbing back to full arousal quicker than he'd thought possible.

"That's right, you scumbag, you bend over and take it. Fuck you! Oh, *fuck!*" Tony's rhythm faltered, and then Chris felt the hot pulse of his cock in his ass as Tony came. Hard, if his groans and shouts were any indication.

The other officer pulled away a moment later, still breathing heavily, and Chris heard him toss something into a wastebasket, and then the clink of his nightstick being returned to its loop. Then Tony unlocked the cuffs, and Chris pushed up from the bed, still weak and shaken from the intense experience.

Tony laughed when he saw Chris's second raging boner of the night. "You really are a fucking pervert, aren't you? Maybe I should call you Bones."

"Anything would be better than Rookie," Chris muttered, only half joking.

It made Tony laugh. "All right, Bones, here's how it'll be. I'm gonna stand here and watch while you take care of that fucking thing, and then we're going to go tell the lovely proprietress good night. And maybe next time I get open-minded while we're on duty, we come back and borrow a room. You good with that?"

Chris swallowed hard as his hand teased along the length of his shaft. His partner smirked down at him, and he stroked, teasing his way from tip to balls and back again. He'd come all right, but this time he'd take his time about it. He was already picturing the day Tony got curious about the other side... "Oh, yeah...I'm good with that."

DICK

Landon Dixon

Detective Taylor shoved the convenience-store door open and walked inside. He was first on the scene. He saw the young black man with the gun pointed at his head and snorted.

"Good collar...Matt," he said, squinting at the clerk's name tag. "You can put the heater down. I got it from here."

Matt, a tall, lanky kid of sixteen, sporting a blond thatch of hair and bright blue eyes, slowly uncocked the fully loaded .44 Magnum with two trembling thumbs. "He thought he could rob me. But I showed him, Officer."

Taylor grunted. "Store policy doesn't call for heroics, Matt. But thanks, all the same." He gripped the perp by his white T-shirt and shook him. "You got a back room, Matt? Somewhere I can view the video footage, give the rubber hose treatment to this scumbag." He grinned, shaking his captive again.

The clerk grinned back, then hustled down the hall at the rear of the store and unlocked a small office for the detective. "Here you go, Officer. Need me to show you how to work the computer?"

Taylor shoved the would-be thief through the door in front of him. "Nah, I can handle it. You take care of the customers. Thanks." He looked at his prisoner, a short, muscular kid of eighteen, with black-velvet skin and sullen brown eyes, a lush mouth and wide nose, close-cropped hair. "If he gets the better of me, I'll give you a holler."

Matt nodded and returned to his post behind the counter at the front of the store. The detective entered the office, closing and locking the door behind him.

"Really bungled this one, huh, Lawrence?"

The kid sat down on the edge of the small, cluttered desk inside the office and wiped his nose with the back of his hand. "How was I supposed to know Blondie out there was Dirty Harry? Like you said, store policy is let 'em have it."

Taylor ran a thick hand through his graying hair. He was forty, going on world-weary, his once rugged body trending toward paunch, the pouches under his gray eyes testimony to too much time on the job, trying to hold things together. It wasn't easy working both sides of the street and keeping from getting caught. He'd been at it since he'd started on the beat, a rookie cop shown the ropes by a friendly, dirty sergeant who had broken him in in more ways than one. He'd been trained in taking it from the street punks in the back alleys, getting it from Sergeant Morrison in the backside. Now, he could give and take with the worst of cops.

"You got nothing, I suppose?" he said to the punk.

"What'd you think?"

"Going to be tough getting you out of this jam...without any payoff."

A cynical grin creased Lawrence's thick lips. Then he went down on his knees in front of Taylor, deftly tugged the detective's fly down and pulled the detective's cock out. The pink appendage was already half-swollen, getting thicker. Lawrence dipped his head down and caught the beefy cap in his mouth and sucked on it.

Taylor jerked at the wet-hot impact of the other's mouth on his sensitive appendage. But he pulled it back out and slapped Lawrence's cheek with it. "Got to give you the rubber hose treatment, remember? For being a bad boy." He slapped Lawrence's other cheek with the stiffening rod.

The kid stared up at him, easily taking the hosing, Taylor's cock briskly beating against his cheeks, brushing past his lips. The detective quickly surged to full erection, striking Lawrence's soft, smooth skin. He dragged the mushroomed head of his dick across the young man's mouth, slowing on the wet, plump lips, then dragging back the other way. Only this time, he stopped his cockhead at Lawrence's open mouth and let it beat there on his lips, basking in the warm, humid breath.

Then he pushed forward, blossoming Lawrence's lips with his knob, shoving his hood inside the kid's mouth. Lawrence sealed his lips around the bloated cap and sucked on it again.

"That's the stuff," Taylor grunted, running his big hands over the young man's head, pulling that head closer, his cock rising up in Lawrence's mouth.

The man on his knees planted his sweaty, pale palms on Taylor's thighs and bobbed his head back and forth. He took the older man's meat right down to the hairy balls, pulled back, tugging tightly, wetly on the surging dong. He'd done it many times before, so he knew exactly what Taylor liked. He sunk his teeth into the blood-engorged shaft just below the hood and made as if he was going to bite the purpled knob right off.

"Fucking right, kid!" Taylor growled, staring down at the teenager with his cockhead between his teeth. "You going to bite the dick that feeds you?" He tingled from head to toe, an aging adrenaline junkie who got his kicks anywhere he could find them now.

Lawrence wagged his head back and forth, pulling Taylor's cock with him, teeth just scratching the surface of shaft. Then he held the man's cock straight, looking up at him, and moved his head slowly forward, swallowing Taylor's prick. Vein-popped shaft glided in between his stretched lips, his mouth consuming more and more over-swollen inches. Until his nose was nuzzling balls again.

Taylor watched, shaking, the depth of the delicious wet heat getting even to him. He pumped his hips, thrusting his hood down Lawrence's velvety throat, fucking the kid's face.

Lawrence's nostrils flared for air, his fingernails digging into Taylor's thighs. But he didn't back off, didn't gag, letting the man saw away at his mouth and throat with that pumped, pulsating cock.

Taylor groaned, plumbing depths of depravity he'd never imagined when he'd first joined the force as a rookie so many years ago. But the temptations had been just too many, the power too absolute. He churned Lawrence's hot mouth, sliding his dick along the young man's slick, beaded tongue. Then he grabbed his cock at the base and ripped it out of the kid's mouth with a pop.

"You going to do better next time?" he rasped, slapping Lawrence's face with his glistening dong.

Lawrence grinned pure white teeth up at the sweating man, showed him the neon-pink cavern of his mouth, the length of his tongue.

Taylor unnoosed the base of his iron-hard rod and stroked. He buckled, semen spurting out of the tip of his prong and striping Lawrence's tongue, shooting into the teenager's mouth. He came hard and heavy in the kid's face, bucking against the closed door of the tiny back room.

Afterward, Taylor escorted Lawrence out of the store and shoved him up against his undercover car to be handcuffed. But the kid jabbed a well-timed elbow into Taylor's gut, doubling the detective over. Lawrence streaked off into the night.

Taylor jammed the clerk's .44 up into the air just in time, before the guy could squeeze off a round. "Don't sweat it," he said. "I'll catch up with him. I don't let these punks get away... for long."

Two convenience stores were knocked over the next week, successfully; the take was small but not insignificant. Taylor waited for Lawrence at their usual rendezvous spot—a darkened doorway in an abandoned projects high-rise—but Lawrence didn't show.

Taylor went on the prowl. He'd seen it before, knew where to look—alleys, parked cars, shitholes. He'd been on the force too long to let one of his boys get the better of him.

He asked around, scouring the 'hoods where delinquents hung out, gangs banged. He rousted fuck-pads and shooting galleries, picking up plenty of illegal drugs and guns on his crusade. It just looked like a righteous cop doing more than his level best to track down a criminal.

Finally, he spotted illicit activity in an alley off Kershaw one lonely night, shone his car light on the sordid scene. It was Lawrence, fucking some punk up the ass, the next downlink in the food chain of survival on the streets.

Taylor gunned the undercover car and roared into the alley, sending the rats and punks scurrying. He barreled out of the vehicle and collared Lawrence by the back of his jeans, as the young man was desperately trying to tug them up so he could run faster.

"Caught with your pants down, huh?" Taylor wheezed, watching the other teenager gazelle down the alley and out the other side. He licked his chops at the sight of those taut, twitching cheeks in the short-shorts. New meat on his beat.

Taylor turned off the light and slammed Lawrence up against the alley wall. "Where's my take from the two scores?" he gritted in the young man's ear.

"I spent it," Lawrence spat back. He tried to spin around, go for Taylor's cock already tenting the front of his pants.

"Uh-uh," Taylor responded, shoving Lawrence back up against the wall. "You owe me more than that. You're going to get what's really coming to you this time."

Lawrence planted his hands up against the grimy wall and wiggled his ass. Taylor yanked the teenager's jeans all the way down, exposing dark, ripe ass mounds. He gripped them, squeezed them, sinking his fingers into the pliable masses. Lawrence groaned.

Taylor unzipped and pulled his baton out of his pants. He was hard as he'd ever been, a back-alley fuck something special. He whacked Lawrence's night-shaded buttocks with his shining pink dong, watching them ripple, feeling them ripple.

"Yeah, fuck me in the ass, pig!" Lawrence hissed, just like the jaded cop liked it.

"Want me to stick your ass, huh, punk?" he rasped in Lawrence's ear, crowding up close to the teenager. He shot his rod in between Lawrence's cheeks, jerking at the smooth, heated sensation, frotting. "Want me to fuck you in the ass, like you deserve?"

Lawrence grunted, undulating his butt back against Taylor's shifting cock.

The detective grabbed a tube of lube out of his jacket pocket, greased his gun and glided it back into Lawrence's bum cleavage, stroking harder. Lawrence tore his hands off the brick and reached back and spread his cheeks. He shuddered as Taylor's slickened hood plugged up against his pucker.

Taylor took a quick glance around, gripping his glistening cannon at the bushy base. No one around to disturb this off-the-record interrogation. He pressed his knob up against Lawrence's bunghole and burst through.

"Fuck!" both men moaned, mushroomed cap muscling through resisting ring.

Taylor leaned into it, shoving his shaft into Lawrence's anus, stuffing the young man with his cock. He went in hard and slow, stretching chute, bumping up against bowels.

The gripping heat made Taylor shake like Lawrence's buttcheeks. He delivered full bore, driving his entire length into the young man's ass, pinning him to the wall, impaling him on his cock. And then he pumped, churning luscious pink sleeve.

"Fuck! Fuck!" Lawrence cried, pounding the alley wall with his clenched fists, anus getting pounded.

Sweat poured off Taylor's brow and ran down his face, his cock consumed by that hot, hungry ass, gliding back and forth in it. He gritted his teeth and moved his hips, fucking faster, harder, his body temperature soaring into the danger zone for a man with his blood-pressure problems.

He drove harder still, gripping Lawrence's hips and slamming up against him over and over. His thighs smacked the young man's cheeks to shuddering, his ramming cock reaming Lawrence's chute, relentlessly, recklessly.

Lawrence was rocked back and forth by the force of the detective's sawing cock in his ass. He moaned, bouncing back, moving his ass in perfect rhythm to Taylor's thrusting, adding to the wicked onslaught.

Taylor didn't have the strength and stamina he'd had as a young cop on the beat. He belted the kid's butt a few more times, then ripped his cock free, squeezing it tight at the base.

Lawrence spun around and assumed the position—on his knees, mouth open. Taylor jammed his throbbing dong into the teenager's mouth and let loose.

"Fuck, yeah!" he howled, bucking, blasting into the steaming maw.

White-hot sperm shot out of the tip of the ruptured cock and rocketed down Lawrence's throat. Taylor jerked, jolted repeatedly by the savage intensity of his orgasm, Lawrence gripping the man's hips, throat working, swallowing all evidence of the depravity.

Taylor shoved the kid up against the side of his vehicle and slapped the handcuffs on him.

"Hey, what the fuck you doing?" Lawrence protested, all the way to the stationhouse.

Taylor looked back at him and grinned. "You shouldn't have tried to screw me over, kid. That's my job. Been doing it for years, and I'm damn good at it."

At the stationhouse, the detective paraded his prisoner in front of his fellow officers. "I think we can close the books on that recent string of convenience store robberies," he said.

Lawrence stared at Taylor, ashen-faced. Then he shot off his mouth, yelling for all to hear, "This cop's dirty. He got a cut of everything I stole! He fucked me in the ass and mouth, too— whole bunch of times!"

Chief of Detectives Morgan laughed, throwing an arm around Taylor's well-rounded shoulders. "How many kids you got at home now, Jim?" he asked.

"Five already and another on the way, Chief," Taylor responded, grinning, thinking of his wife, Trudy. She'd been one of his "girls" when he'd first started out on the beat, a rookie cop racking up some freebies. Until he'd taken care of her.

BROKEN IN
AT THE BIG
HOUSE

K. Vale

Wakey, wakey." The voice melded with the dream. A shadowed face Will knew to be his best friend Dwayne from high school spoke the cryptic message. For some reason, Dream Dwayne was at the training academy with Will. It didn't make sense, but Will was enjoying the illusion. The fantasy of Dwayne sitting on Will's feet as he curled upward to perform the required sit-ups for the agility test was arousing. *I'm getting hard.* He could nearly feel his buddy's weight pressing down on his legs, firm hands on his knees. But what the hell was Dwayne talking about?

"Rise and shine, Rookie."

Will snorted and the tendrils of dream spun away. His eyelids flickered open and reality slammed into him like a freight train full of bricks.

Shit! I'm at work! Caught sleeping on the freakin' job!

Such an offense wasn't taken lightly, Will knew from various hazing horror stories passed around at the coffee station. A sleeping guard not only put himself at risk, but also the rest of the correctional officers on duty. And it wasn't as if Will had been there for years, built up a reputation and made friends. He was the new guy on cell block B, and it took a while before any of the old-timers let fresh meat into their circle of pals.

I am so screwed.

Sergeant Evan Delaney's hands were planted above Will's knees as he leaned down to speak face-to-face.

"You haven't been here long enough to get away with shit like that, boy. What happens when I report you to the captain?"

The sergeant's face was rugged. His sharp cheekbones and square jaw were almost too severe but were tempered by the lushness of his lips. Will stared at the generous mouth as the man reprimanded him.

"Please don't write me up. I swear I won't do it again. It was just...I'm having work done in my bathroom, and the plumber was in today. I couldn't get any sleep and after three nights on..."

"Maybe you should think about scheduling your plumber to come on your days off, Rookie."

"I will. I mean...next time. I promise it won't happen again. Please don't..." Will felt like a parrot, repeating the same inane phrase in a pathetic loop. The sleep-spawned semi-erection in his work blues lay heavy against his leg as a testament to his mistake. Dwayne had gotten Will hard on more than one occasion, not that Will had ever admitted his lust to his friend.

Being caught shirking his duty should have scared Will soft, but his dick continued to throb in his pants like a heat-seeking missile in need of defusing.

Those lips. Will had never felt particularly attracted to white guys before, but this big man, pinning him with an intense hazel gaze and licking his full lips in an oddly suggestive manner, had Little Will's undivided attention.

"Maybe we can make some kind of arrangement. Hard to squeal if I've got something in my mouth, you know what I mean?" Evan's hands slid up Will's inner thighs. The fingertips on the guard's right hand grazed the head of Will's hard-on.

Holy shit! Am I hearing this right? It reeked of blackmail, and yet Will's body buzzed with excitement. The prospect of paying for Evan's silence with sex seemed too good to be true.

"What do you...?" Will swallowed the massive lump in his throat. "What do I need to do to keep you quiet?"

Evan's mesmerizing mouth pinched up in a wicked half smile. He knew he had Will by the balls.

Does he have any idea how turned on I am? He doesn't seem the least bit worried about me accusing him of sexual harassment. Of using his rank to make me do whatever he wants. Bend over and take his cock deep in my ass. Suck his balls dry.

Fuck. Will's dick pulsed painfully and he felt precome dampen his boxers.

"Boy, I don't want you to keep me quiet," the big man nearly whispered. "You're gonna have to make me scream to wipe this one off your record."

Cell block F, once a geriatric unit, had been closed since the budget cuts of '07. Michigan's governor had hacked away at correctional funding, and the prison had responded with layoffs, releases of nonviolent criminals, and general unease. Hiring dropped off, but the hands of time never stopped. People retired. One guard even died of a heart attack while on duty. Ever so slowly, new slots opened, but the fact was Will was lucky as hell to have this job.

Am I jeopardizing it worse by meeting Sergeant Delaney in an abandoned bathroom?

He knew the answer was probably yes, but it didn't stop him from furtively looking around the abandoned hall and then unlocking the heavy iron door. Its hinges were ghostly silent and Will had a sudden notion that perhaps they were well oiled. Well used. Had this gate led to countless clandestine meetings?

He squeezed through, thinking of oil and erections, wondering if he was about to be initiated into some exquisitely sordid club. He felt as if he was making a memory, one that would leave him waking from future dreams, his pulse pounding with insane terror and his cock unbearably stiff. One he would jerk off to for years to come.

His dick led the way to the unused staff bathroom.

The light was off, and Will initially thought he had beat Evan there. He reached for the switch and flicked it up, but darkness reigned.

"Lock the door and come here." The gruff voice echoed in the cold space, and a shiver dominoed down Will's spine, brittle and delicious. His breath seemed to be racing his heartbeat.

He twisted the lock obediently. Clearing his throat, he stepped forward, one hand outstretched and the other gliding over the tiled wall for direction.

The ceramic dropped off under his fingers, and Will was lost in a sea of black. When strong arms wrapped around him, grabbed his wrists and forced them over his head, he felt like his lifeboat had arrived. He was backed into a hard surface by an equally unyielding body. He couldn't help but notice the thick wood that lined up perfectly with his own, stroked back and forth as their legs moved.

A mouth, full and insistent, met his lips. They pressed together—sweet-soft flesh surrounded by next-morning bristles—and tasted each other until the need for more prevailed. Will stuck a tentative tongue out and was met by a hot swirl of hungry muscle. It filled his mouth, his head, his senses. He moaned, loud and long, as Evan's granite piece surged up into him, grinding to the beat of his tongue.

"Fuck." He spat the word as he pulled away. "Want me to suck you?"

"Mmm." The growl was an assent. A directive. A total fucking turn-on, and Will dropped to his knees, fumbling with belt and hardware with desperately clumsy fingers. Finally, hot skin prodded his cheek, and relief flooded his body as he sucked in the velvet head, gulped down inch after inch like a famished man. He pulled back and barked a laugh at the thick string of drool that accompanied the act. He was salivating like a fucking Pavlovian dog.

That's right. Tell me you're gonna fuck me, and then make me finish half an eight-hour shift. You bet I'm fuckin' droolin'.

He slurped spit and cock back in, twisting a lubed choke hold at the base of his sergeant's prick while he lavished the head with attention.

As Will bobbed and pulled, he slicked wet fingers back over the man's perineum, massaging in time with his mouth. He backed up on the thick cock and fluttered his tongue over the tip until the sergeant gave a raspy groan and pulled him to his feet.

Invisible hands slid over Will's trousers, freed his cock. The sound of Evan spitting was a precursor to the slippery hand that began to jerk him.

"Ahhh…" Will let out a harsh breath as he pumped his hips against the tight fist. He felt his partner shift his body and force Will's backside against a cold, hard ridge. *Sink counter.* His ass was pushed onto it, his leg lifted against solid shoulder, and then Evan's lips wrapped around him.

I knew they would feel amazing.

Swiveling mouth and flicking tongue, a hand that slid up to corkscrew over his glossy tip in a fluid motion, all left his legs trembling. A flat, wet tongue lapped from the underside of his balls to his helmet in quick lollypop-licking strokes. Over and over, Evan's mouth massaged him from taint to frenulum until Will thought his body might melt and run down the drain.

"I'm gonna fuck this tight ass. Teach you to fall asleep on the job, Rookie. Get up and turn around."

Will's legs were rubber, but he peeled his butt off the counter and did as he was told, all the while praying he wouldn't squirt the second Evan's dick touched his hot hole.

"Hands on the faucet and keep 'em there."

Will leaned over and groped for the sink. He found the icy metal shaft and wrapped his fingers around it.

In the dark, Will's senses hummed like an electric current. He was on high alert from his ears, to his aching dick, to his toes curled up in nervous anticipation.

There was the feather of air against the back of his legs and a fleeting kiss of skin as Evan moved. Noise tantalized him from behind. The crinkle of a condom being unwrapped. The heavy drop of clothing as it hit the floor. An odd jingling.

Was it possible to come from sound alone?

A warm hand slid down his arm, checked to be certain he'd followed the directions of his superior. Something rigid and smooth wrapped around one wrist, and then the other. The cuffs clicked into place.

Will let out a strangled cry. Fear and unparalleled desire spiked through him and shot out of his mouth.

"Lock you up like a bad boy." Sergeant Delaney breathed hotly against his neck. "Spit in my hand, Rookie." The fingers, sour with latex, thick and calloused, toyed with his lips and

Will fought against his suddenly dry mouth to procure the lubricant.

And then, sweet fuck, the prodding at his door came. Insistent nudging made him spread his legs farther apart in welcome. Those scratchy hands kneaded his cheeks, worked them around Evan's fat head as it poked against him and finally popped in. A slow slide filled him completely, watered his eyes and stole his breath. He was light-headed. Will finally sucked in a lungful and followed it with a guttural sigh. Evan started slow and silent, but built to swift strokes and heavy panting. The slick push and pull seemed to flood Will's senses and then leave him wanting. Begging. He was surprised to realize the "Please. Please. Please," whimpered over and over was his own. He hadn't realized he was even speaking.

Fingers bit into Will's hips as the sergeant rode up on him. The weight drove him down while the guy fucked into his ass like an animal compelled by instinct. Loud grunts accompanied each thrust as the man-beast took Will from behind.

"Yeah. You like that?" He growled. "Like my cock pounding you? You gonna fall asleep again, boy?"

"Yes. Yes. Yes," Will chanted to the rhythm of Evan's cock. *Was the answer supposed to be no?* For this, he would fake sleeping on the job. His head thumped against what must have been a mirror as the big dude drilled him. The counter scraped the underside of his cock. He would have loved a warm hand wrapped around it, but it didn't matter. The small bite of pain added to the frenzy ballooning inside him. And that glorious dick slamming the back of his balls from the inside was easily going to finish him off.

"So fuckin' tight. So fuckin' tight." Evan hissed it again and again through clenched teeth behind Will's ear. The pressure in Will's nuts crested, near agony and all pleasure as the first spasm jolted every muscle in his body. He shuddered. The orgasm ripped through his insides before it washed across his belly, warmed the chilly porcelain. Evan recognized his cries or maybe the periodic clamping of his ass as he emptied his sac. He followed Will's lead. The man gave a mighty thrust and with a muffled yell fell trembling against Will's back, pulsing jerkily into him as the rush subsided.

Will's heart rate slowed. The cool of the vanity seeped into his awareness. Sergeant Delaney let out a sigh and finally pulled out and away. Will released his white-knuckle grip, slid the cuffs over the spigot, and stood. He stretched his stiff back, waiting for what came next. He prayed it wasn't him asking for handcuff keys at the main desk and being summarily fired.

The whisper of fabric teased in the darkness, and then a faint tinkling sound. Warm sandpaper hands reached out to him, felt their way to the keyhole and set him free.

"Welcome to Monroe State Pen. Lookin' forward to working with ya." A sharp slap on Will's bare ass startled a small shriek from him. He heard Evan chuckle as the sound of feet moved away. A blade of dim light shone and was swallowed again by darkness as the door opened and closed. Will was alone.

"You still here?" Officer Grayson sat in the control booth and eyed Will curiously.

"Ahh, just got caught shootin' the shit with some of the guys. Decent crew we've got working here," Will said with a sincere smile.

"Yeah." Grayson nodded. "I told ya you'd fit in. All that worry during training for nothing, huh?"

"Guess so," Will said. "Have a good shift."

"Hey, thanks. Get some rest, buddy."

A little sore and a lot sticky under his rumpled uniform, Will walked out to his car with a grin that wouldn't let up.

His bed was calling to him. He could hardly wait to curl up under his comforter and sleep the day away. Somehow, he knew once he closed his eyes, a luscious set of lips would be starring in his dreams.

FLIGHT 1769

Max Vos

U.S. marshals were a pain in the ass to deal with. Direct flights into and out of Washington, DC must have two U.S. marshals on board. That is the law since 9/11. With three direct outbound flights a day to DC and three inbound flights, which means six sets of U.S. marshals, there's nothing to do but deal with it.

They must be escorted from the crew rooms to the aircraft before passenger boarding begins and escorted off the planes after all passengers are deplaned. So someone has to stop what he's doing and walk those guys into the crew rooms. Working as a ramp rat—the guys you see running around outside around the airplanes—in a small airport is difficult enough, without having to stop to escort those guys around.

Now some might say that it isn't that big a deal, but when you are dealing with a tight timeline, and only have fifteen minutes turnaround time from landing to takeoff of the next flight, it is a big deal, especially for a small airport. Luckily that only happens once a day; the other two flights are one first thing in the morning, and an overnighter. The best scenario is when the midday flight keeps the same set of marshal's to make the flight back. That happens less than half the time though.

Taking a shift for a buddy whose wife had surgery that day, I was pulling a double, and closing. The last flight in was the DC flight. It also so happens that we were already one man short of the five-man crew that normally worked closing. The rest of the crew let me work operations that night, since it was the easiest job, taking pity on me since I'd already worked a full shift doing cargo/baggage, though with being one man short I was also going out between flights to help clean planes as they came in.

"Tyson, Tyson flight 1769 inbound, five minutes out," the radio crackled.

"Flight 1769, copy, five minutes out, see you on the ground, 1769," I responded.

Since the other three guys were in the ramp room, where everyone sat around in between flights, I didn't need to call it out on the ramp radio; I just went in and told them.

"I'll park 'em and get the marshals up," I volunteered.

The others just nodded and we all went out to wait on the DC flight. Opening the door the heat just about knocked me over. It has been one of the hottest summers on record, and the tarmac held all the heat of the day, radiating up, even at ten at night.

Grabbing the lighted wands, I took position waiting on the ERJ to pull around the corner. Hearing the jet, I flicked on the wands, and marshaled in the plane. Chuck got the air stairs set, Tim pulled up with the baggage cart, Peter got the belt loader pulled up, opened up the cargo bin and started off-loading baggage.

This being a small airport, the passengers would come down

the air stairs and walk across the tarmac about fifty feet into the terminal. I greeted passengers and made sure that all carry-on checked bags were available before they went inside. Once all passengers had deplaned and gotten inside, I waited for the U.S. marshals.

Normally there was a veteran and a rookie, one being older and one being younger. All U.S. marshals on flights were under the age of forty, so there wasn't a lot of age difference most of the time. I didn't mind the marshals all that much since all of them were in tip-top shape and usually good looking. This time was no exception.

They started down the air stairs; each had a rolly-four, the type and size of carry-on bag, one black and one dark green. One marshal was older, with a blond crew cut, tight-clipped mustache, and shoulders the size of a refrigerator. The younger marshal raked his hand through dark wavy hair, not as broad as his partner, but still pretty wide in the shoulders. Each had suit coats on, the standard uniform for these guys. I felt for them having to wear them in this heat.

"Evening gentlemen, if you'll follow me I'll take you up to the terminal," I said, greeting them.

"Thanks. Damn it's hot here," the senior officer remarked, wiping his brow.

"Yeah, sorry man, it's been the hottest summer I can remember." What else was I going to say?

Escorting the two officers up to the main terminal I bid them good night then went back to help out the rest of the crew. Once downstairs Pete told me that they were all done with the plane, so the only thing left for me to do was print out the final paperwork, file it and go home. This was good news. I wasn't looking forward to cleaning that plane in this heat. I said good night to the rest of the guys, saying I'd lock up and they were free to go on home. Finished a few minutes later, I turned out the lights, locked the door and hightailed it out of there.

After working seventeen hours, most of it in the heat, I was damned tired. The only thing I wanted right then was a cold beer, a shower and my bed. Seeing as I had the next three days off I decided I'd hit the bar at the airport hotel, which just so happened to be between me and the employee parking lot. Isn't that convenient?

I walked into the airport hotel lounge and went right to the bar. The only other customers in there were the two air marshals from the DC flight. Knowing that the restaurant dining room closed at nine, they each had a sandwich from the kitchen and a beer. That told me that they were not going to be the crew that went out on the early morning flight, or they would be breaking the law by drinking this close to flight time. I'm sure that they weren't that dumb, so I guessed that they'd be doing the midday flight. I tipped my hat to them, being the Southern gentleman that I am, in greeting, and ordered a beer, chugging half of it. There really is nothing better than an ice-cold beer when it's so hot out.

Before I could finish off the beer I saw the older officer leave while his partner was still at a table. Just as I was about to order another beer the rookie marshal stepped up to the bar and asked if he could join me, running his hand through that dark wavy hair of his. Of course nothing would suit me better—having a hot cop keeping me company.

We each ordered another beer, same kind. He took a small sip and then licked his almost too pink, full lips. I noticed that he had a pretty heavy five o'clock shadow working, which only highlighted his very kissable looking lips. While I watched him he turned and looked at me. I know I gasped. His eyes were purple. He smiled at me with dazzling white teeth. Where the fuck did this guy come from?

"Where ya from?" Might as well ask the guy.

"New York. Bronx," he answered after taking a swig from his beer.

"Ah, a Yankee, unless you move here and then you're a damn Yankee," I smiled at him.

After scowling at me a moment he asked, "Is that a good thing or a bad thing?"

Was this guy flirting with me? "I guess that depends on who you ask."

"I'm asking you," he shot back instantly, catching me completely off guard.

"Ummm...well..." I stammered.

He laughed knowing he'd got me. His laugh was deep and throaty, giving me a tingle behind the fly of my work shorts.

"So would it be such a bad thing if I lived here?" he asked leaning toward me a little.

I could smell him he was so close, and it was intoxicating. There was no doubt that he was flirting with me.

"Whatcha got to bring to the table?" I could play this game; I knew it well.

Without blinking an eye he said, "How about one-hundred-percent-pure hot Italian blood?"

"Don't know that they categorize blood by ethnicity over at the blood bank, but we can always use a decent pizza joint," I pounded back.

"Touché!" he said as he raised his beer in a toast. After taking a drink he stuck out his hand. "Anthony Pucelli; you can call me Tony, my friends call me...often."

Damn, but he was forward. I just raised my eyebrows, then pulled on my beer, not replying.

"Is there anything interesting to do around here? Looks as if I'm stuck here until the day after tomorrow," Tony asked.

"How'd that happen? You guys are normally only here overnight, if that, right?" I asked surprised.

"Something about switching out crews from what I understand. My partner and I are being split up. He's going out on the midday flight tomorrow; I don't go out until the morning flight the day after tomorrow." He shrugged as he took a drink of his nearly finished beer. "There's even talk of opening an office here since there are so many DC flights out, and from here we can get to any major hub of any airline. They're asking for volunteers to move here. Of course, this being my rookie year, it's possible that I might be transferred somewhere whether I like it or not. Sometimes it's just better to volunteer so you do have a choice."

"Um, not to be offensive or anything, but you're a little older than most of the rookies I see with the marshals office." I said.

"Yeah, well I came in directly from the Marines after doing two tours in Iraq. I'd had enough of that shit. I got tired of someone always trying to shoot my ass." Tony didn't seem at all happy remembering.

"Ah well, I guess I can see your point there," I commiserated.

"I guess I'm looking for a change. This isn't the highest-paying gig, and New York isn't exactly a cheap place to live. Besides my family is driving me nuts pushing me to get married and settle down." Tony was peeling away the label on his beer. "I'm not really the marrying kind of guy, if you know what I mean."

"Oh? And that would be because...?" I asked, trying to feel him out a little more.

He didn't answer. Well, verbally that is. Tony looked at me

with such intensity that I started to get a little warm and that tingle in my groin started again. One thing about this guy, he sure wasn't shy.

"Let me buy you another beer," he said, as he was trying to get the bartender's attention.

"I can't, I have to be able to drive home. Two is my limit, but thanks anyway," I answered.

"I can *drive* you," Tony leered at me, making me shiver a bit.

"Oh? I don't know about that. You know what they say about Marines."

"And what would that be?" he asked me.

"They're all bottoms." If he was gay I knew that would get a rise out of him. If he wasn't gay he would get pissed off.

"Not all. I'm kind of a flip-flop-and-fly kind of guy myself. I can drive or be driven." Again with that killer smile, but with eyes that could set a barn on fire in no time. "So why not have another beer and see who's a better pilot?"

The time of truth: I'm not usually the type to jump into bed after just meeting a guy. Not my style really. However here was this Italian hunk who was more than a little interested in me, asking me, quite bluntly, to have sex with him. Who was I to look a gift horse in the mouth?

Without my even answering him, Tony ordered us each another beer. I couldn't decide if this Italian stallion was cocky, overconfident or what, but it didn't seem as if he was going to take no for an answer. What the hell, live and let live. Besides, those eyes were enough to make me wonder what the rest of him was going to look like.

As we drank our beers, we chatted, getting to know each other a little. Seems Tony came from a large Italian family with three brothers and three sisters. He was second-genera-tion American, his parents still spoke Italian. He made it clear that he loved his family, but might love them a little more long distance.

We each finished our beers, and with a nod of his head toward the door I followed Tony to the lobby and into an elevator. He selected the floor and turned to me, leaning against the wall of the elevator, a hand on either side of my shoulders.

"Damn you are cute," he breathed at me.

"You're kinda hot yourself, but I think you know that already," I grinned up at him.

Tony had to be six feet tall to my measly five-eight, dark to my blond. We were opposites in many ways. The elevator dinged, doors opened and I followed Tony to his room.

Once past the door of his room, Tony grabbed me behind the neck, pulled me to him and laid a passion-filled kiss on me that was entirely too brief. I soon understood why when he took off his jacket, unholstered his gun and put it in the room's safe. Then he turned to me and kissed me senseless.

Breaking away, I said I needed a shower, explaining my day of sweating my ass off.

"Yeah, a shower sounds like a good idea," Tony whispered in my ear, giving me the shivers again.

I started to unbutton my uniform shirt, "Here...let me, please?" Tony asked.

I shrugged and he slowly unbuttoned my shirt, staring into my eyes the entire time. Once he had the shirt off, he unbuckled my airline-issued belt. Still looking intently into my eyes, he undid my shorts, pulled down the zipper and reached around, pushing his hands underneath my shorts and grasping my ass in his meaty hands.

Gently pushing me back onto the bed, he kneeled and pulled off my shoes, socks and my shorts that had pooled around my ankles. That left me in nothing but an old jockstrap that I wore when it was so stifling hot. I guess he approved from the noise coming from him, something between a moan and a growl. If I had any doubt, his crawling up between my legs and sniffing real hard with his nose buried in my crotch did away with that.

I know I'm not too hard on the eyes. My body is real tight from working on the ramp, lifting bags all the time and sweating my butt off in the summer; having a very active job kept me very fit, and I was naturally muscular. I had little to no body hair on my upper body, and very perky nipples that also were extremely sensitive. My legs were one of my best features, thick, all muscle and covered with white-blond hair. I was a little more than average endowed, neatly circumcised.

Tony stood suddenly and started undressing. I've never seen anyone get naked as fast as this man; it was like watching a tornado. He pulled me to my feet, tugged me into the bathroom and started the shower, never saying a word. Turning to me he hooked a finger on either side of my hips, pushing the jock down. Stooping over he lifted each foot, completely removing the undergarment. Wadding it up, he brought it to his face and inhaled deeply, with his eyes closed. When he opened those violet eyes they were on fire, looking at me like I was lunch, giving me another shiver.

Checking the temperature of the shower, he stepped in, holding out his hand to me. He grabbed a bar of soap and this hot Italian man began to wash me, not leaving an inch untouched, making me feel treasured. Only thing I could do was stand there, enjoy it and enjoy the sight of this beautiful man.

Was there such a thing as a typical Italian look? If so he was it. Beautiful olive skin, his chest covered in dark fur. His nipples were the color of ripe plums; he had shoulders and biceps a sculptor would envy. Powerful legs also covered in dark hair and what had to be the most perfect penis I'd ever seen. And he was totally into me? Cool!

Once he was done I snapped the soap out of his hand and turned him around, pushing him so that his arms were bracing him against the wall of the shower. Starting with his near-perfect shoulders I washed him, slowly moving down, massaging as I went until I got to the small of his back. The sight of his tight furry ass made my mouth water and my hands itch, in anticipation of touching the firm round globes.

Tony was softly moaning under my ministrations, massaging him as I washed. Pushing between the cheeks of his delectable ass elicited a sigh as he pushed into my manipulating hands. Touching his legs, lathering them up was a total joy to me. What can I say? I'm a leg man.

Turning him around, I started on the front side. If I thought the backside was good, the front side was out of this world. Lifting his arms to wash his pits, I encountered the hairiest armpit I think I'd ever seen. There is just something about a manly armpit that makes me purr. His hairy chest and stomach made my dick so hard it hurt. Tony was also fully erect as I washed his genitals.

He and I were about the same size, dickwise, but the coloring couldn't have been more different, with me being pink tones and him being plum colored. The head of his dick was pure perfection. He may have been a little thicker than I, but if so, it wasn't by much. I was so in awe of him—his physical being—that I think I would have been happy just washing him. Well...maybe not.

Looking up into his face, I saw that he was smiling at me, watching me washing him. "Enjoying yourself?" he asked.

"Very much so." I knew I was blushing as I answered him.

"Good, because I enjoyed washing you just as much, I believe," he said before lightly kissing me.

After turning the water off, we both dried off quickly, our urgency pushing the need for each other. Pulling me onto the bed with him, Tony quickly took charge, pinning my arms above my head as he ravaged my mouth, leaving rub burns from the stubble of his thick heavy beard. His kiss was sloppy wet, full of passion and need.

Moving down my body, tasting, nibbling, paying special attention to my ultrasensitive nipples, nearly sending me through the roof, he finally made it to my drooling, dripping cock. When I thought I was finally going to find some relief to my aching dick, he completely bypassed it, going for my tight balls instead.

He slobbered over my almost-blue balls, manipulating them and leaving me breathing so hard I thought my lungs were going to heave out of my chest. Seizing me behind my knees, he lifted my ass in the air and zeroed in on my hole, like a missile to its target, causing me to yell out at the attack. His licking, sucking, biting, and rubbing his chin stubble across my hole had me squirming uncontrollably in short order.

Jumping up, Tony went to his carry-on bag, grabbed a small kit from inside and dumped the contents on the bed. Lube, condoms and poppers tumbled out. He quickly tore open a condom with his teeth, rolled it on, lubed up his near-purple dick, slicked up my hole, threw my legs over his shoulders and took aim.

Looking at me with fire in his eyes, which now were a deep-purple velvet, a lascivious grin on his built-for-sex lips, he gently pushed until the perfect head of his dick popped through. It having been a while since I had last been fucked, the pain was sharp, causing me to gasp and clench my eyes shut for a moment. Being patient, Tony waited for me to adjust to him entering me.

Slowly the pain subsided, replaced with a burning of desire. My hands on his hips, I pulled him slowly forward, impaling me, inch by inch until his thick pubic bush was scrubbing underneath my balls. I felt completely stuffed, like a Thanksgiving turkey, pleasantly so.

Leaning over me, Tony kissed me deeply, almost doubling me in half, constricting my breathing. Letting my legs slip down to wrap around his waist, Tony continued to kiss me deeply, while starting to slowly pump in and out of my stretched ass with short strokes. It wasn't long before I was moaning, wanting more action. Sensing my need, slowly Tony picked up the pace until he was drilling my ass with long deep strokes.

With him slamming into me hard, long-dicking me with every stroke, hitting my prostate, there was no way I was going to last. Pushing up on his arms, his lust-driven gaze piercing me—his furry stomach smashing, rubbing my oozing, throbbing dick sent me over the edge. My hands clenching his biceps, I screamed silently, my head thrown back. I could feel the muscles in my ass clamp down on his thrusting cock, as I pulsed out what felt like gallons of my pent-up spunk.

Starting as a low growl that grew into a low roar, Tony reached his own orgasm, thrusting deep into my gut, pushing mine to last even longer. I was able to open my eyes to catch the last few seconds of Tony blasting away deep inside me. He was beautiful in the throes of passion, corded muscle straining his neck, pectoral muscles bulging, flushed with a sheen of sweat covering his body, making him glow.

Collapsing on top of me, breathing heavily, he started kissing my neck, nuzzling behind my ear with something that was between a hum and a purr. Slowly he withdrew his semi-hard cock from me and rolled to the side, pulling me with him. Looking deep into my eyes he reached up and stroked my hair, my neck and then my lips with the tip of his thumb. Slowly, eyes wide open, he gently kissed me.

With arms and legs intertwined, we both fell asleep. I awoke sometime later with Tony making love to me. It was nothing like before; it was slow, tender but intense. With me covered in cum yet again, we fell asleep.

The sun was up and peeking through the slight opening in the drapes, slicing across the bed, and I was able to see this handsome man only inches from my face. Slowly his eyes opened, again surprising me with the color. A slow, lazy smile turning into a grin, changed his face, making me smile in return.

"Morning, handsome. Do you have any idea how beautiful you are?" Tony whispered.

"Me? I was thinking the same about you," I huffed back, my voice still raspy from just waking up.

"Think we can stay in bed all day?" The way he asked, I knew he was serious and incredibly enough, a little anxious, like I might say no.

"I need to get up...just long enough to find out where to get those transfer papers for you," I said, grinning at him.

"Now that we can do," Tony answered, smiling brightly.

THIS
CHARMING
MAN

Shane Allison

I could barely keep my eyes open. All I wanted to do was take a shower, get some food in my stomach and take my ass to bed. I took the truck route way home to avoid all the traffic lights. I prayed that I wouldn't fall asleep at the wheel as I put miles of road behind me. *Damn, it's foggy tonight.* When I heard Rihanna's "Rude Boy" starting to play on the radio, I turned it up, blasting her sexy-ass voice in my piece-of-shit Buick. "Oh, this my jam, right here," I said, and sang along. It was all I needed to wake me up. I was probably fuckin' the words up but I didn't care. I controlled the car with my left hand as I snapped my fingers to Rihanna's jam with my right. I had both my windows down, acting like I was the only one on the stretch of fogged road. I was car-dancing my ass off. As I was working my upper body to the song, I was startled by the red, blue and white lights flashing in my rearview. "Ah, shit." I turned down the radio, bringing Rihanna to a whisper. "Damn, was I speeding?" I pulled into the empty parking lot of the Koger Center. My registration was in the glove compartment and I had just paid the car insurance for that month so I was good.

I pulled into a parking space, killed the engine and stuck both hands out of the window. I didn't want to give these redneck pig-cops a reason. I tried to figure out what I was being stopped for. "If I do get a ticket, he's going to take half the damn night to write it up." I heard the door of the cop car shut. I heard footsteps drawing closer, saw the gleam from a flashlight.

"Driver's license, registration and insurance, please," the cop asked. It was a brother, thank-fuckin' god. A sense of relief washed over me. I reached in the front pocket of my pants and pulled out my wallet.

"Take your license out for me, please?" he asked.

"I sure can," I said, politely. Sometimes if you're nice and you cooperate, they will let you go with a warning. I pulled out my license and handed it to the officer. I reached over and pulled open the latch of the glove compartment and took out my insurance card and registration from between my phone charger, other miscellaneous papers and a can of air freshener, and handed him the rest of what he asked for.

"Do you know why I stopped you?"

"No, was I speeding?"

"You ran that stop sign a quarter mile back."

I was so into the music, I hadn't realized.

"Oh, I'm sorry, man. I can't see nothin' out here in this fog."

"Just sit tight for me."

The cop went back to his car. He looked familiar.

I knew he didn't believe me when I told him that I didn't see a stop sign. I mean, damn, look at this fog. I can barely see my hand in front of my face. A two-hundred-dollar ticket was the last thing I needed.

It didn't take him long to come back.

"Hey, I didn't put two and two together when I looked at your license, but did you by any chance go to James Baldwin High?" the cop asked.

"Yeah, class of nineteen-ninety-two."

"I graduated the same year as you!"

I peered out of the car window to get a better look.

"Alan? Alan Williamson?"

"Yeah, what's up?"

"Ah, man, damn," I grinned, opening the car door.

We gave each other a big bear hug.

Being that Tallahassee is so small, I wasn't that surprised to run into him.

"Man, you scared the hell out of me."

"I thought this car looked familiar."

"Yeah, man. I've been at work all day, covered a shift for a friend of mine."

"I hear ya. I just started my shift. I got another five hours out here."

The last time I laid eyes on Alan, he was working as an usher at one of the local art-house movie theaters. It was weird seeing him in a cop uniform, but he looked good, and was still cute as all get out.

"So how long has it been, like—"

"Seven years," I said. "I see you traded in those ugly-ass paisley vests at the movie theater for a police uniform, huh? Look at you, got a gun and everything."

"I just finished up at the academy. I got a job right out with the department. Derrick, that shit was hard at first and I didn't think I would get through it. They tell you in the catalog that it's only six months but it was more like a year with all the classes and exams you have to take and the physical shit they have you doin'."

"I was about to say. You've lost a lot of weight. You look good." *Even after all these years,* I thought.

"I lost like thirty pounds. They don't play. They run it like a boot camp."

"Bein' a cop looks good on you," I said, leaning against my car with my arms folded.

Alan still had that basketball player build from high school along with the same coffee-cream-brown skin tone, with a short haircut that was faded off to the sides. His smile was big, pretty and white. Alan always did have a nice smile. I hope he didn't think I was just talking out of my ass just to get out of a ticket.

"So where you work at?"

"I work for the state, but you know how that is. It's just for right now until I go back to school."

"Masters?"

"PhD."

"Do it, man. Not a lot of brothers are getting their PhDs."

"Thanks, man. You should tell my mama that. 'You'll be in your forties by the time you finish. Ain't nobody gonna hire you at forty-somethin'-years old.'"

"I went into the academy at thirty-eight and they hired me. Age ain't nothin' but a number, man."

Alan smelled good as hell but I couldn't place the cologne.

"Tell ya what. I will let you off with a warning if you have dinner with me tomorrow night."

Was this really happening? Was this some kind of dream, 'cause this kind of shit doesn't happen to me in Tallahassee. Alan Williamson, voted James Baldwin High School's Most Valuable Football Player of 1992, was asking me out on a date? What strange, bizarre world had I just stumbled into? I just looked at Alan. It was like I was staring clean through him.

"We could do it another time if you have plans," Alan said.

I heard his words, but I was in a dazed state.

"Hey, Earth...Earth to Derrick?"

"Naw, I'm cool. I'm off tomorrow, so no, no plans."

"I get off duty around seven. How about we meet up at that new bar and grill on North Monroe. The End Zone. Have you ever been there?"

"No. I've only passed by it a few times."

"So, we meet there about eight o'clock?" Alan asked.

"I'll be there."

Alan handed me back my wallet, registration and insurance card.

"Oh, let's exchange numbers in case we need to call," said Alan.

He handed me a business card with his cell phone number scribbled on it. I plucked a pen and an old grocery receipt from the drink coaster and jotted down my number. I usually have a rule about giving my number to guys. I don't. Period. But I made an exception for Alan.

"It was good seein' you again," I said, smiling.

"You too, man. Get home safe."

I woke up the next morning with the biggest grin across my fat, round face, as if I had just won a five-day, six-night vacation. Alan still looked the same—smokin' hot still after all these years. I had the biggest crush on him in school. I used to sit in a corner in the school library and write sappy love poems about him in this old purple notebook. I still have it, I think, buried in a box somewhere under a stack of books. I was invisible until he approached me one day in the library and asked me to tutor him. He walked in like he had never been inside a library before. I stared at him like he was some kind of celebrity waxwork but would look down whenever he looked in my direction. He was looking for me. "Derrick?" he said, like he wasn't sure it was me.

"Hey, what's up?"

"Mrs. Kanu said you tutor."

From that day on we were cool. Alan didn't seem to care that I was gay or what people would think if he hung out with me. I went from zero to eighty flat in the popular kid social circle. I was getting invited to all the parties, and all the guys that used to give me wedgies and lock me in the field house for kicks, were suddenly my bff's. I mean I knew they were only kissing my ass because of Alan, but I didn't care. There was no way I was going to go back to being a nobody once I became a somebody. I didn't find out that Alan was into guys until a drunken night at Jatari Booker's party. His parents were off on an African vacation. Alan and I were both fucked up. Alan and I started hooking up after school while his folks were still at work. He was actually the first boy I kissed.

I got jealous when he started going out with Jalea, one of the cheerleaders, but we didn't stop messing around. We agreed on a system where he would leave a note in my locker telling me that it was cool to come over if Jalea wasn't around, which she always was, so I started spending less and less time at his parents' place. Alan was the first boy I fell in love with, but 'til this day, he didn't know it.

The night of the dinner, I started getting ready around six. I jumped in the shower and made sure everything was clean, especially my asshole and balls. I was primping and preening like some bubbly prom queen. I looked at the clock on my bedside table. It read 7:15. "Damn, I'm gonna be late."

I put on a pair of 501s I had just gotten out of the cleaners. I was trying to decide between a corduroy shirt that still had the tag on it and a purple Polo I bought from Diamondnaire's, this new store on the south side of town.

"It's too damn hot for corduroy," I said, so I decided on the Polo, which went better with dark-blue jeans anyway. I took a long look at myself in my bedroom mirror. There wasn't a hair out of place. The last time I went on a date I was twenty-three, and it was a catastrophe with a capital C. I slapped on some Halston Z-14 for a final touch, careful not to put on too much. As I stuffed my size thirteens into a pair of Timberlands, my phone rang.

"That's probably Alan wanting to know if I'm on my way."

I flipped my phone open.

"Damn, it's Shakeema. I don't have time for her nosy ass right now."

"Hello?"

"How's my favorite gay doing?"

I can't stand it when she calls me *her* gay like I'm something small enough to carry around in her Gucci knockoff.

"Hey, what's up?"

"Don't tell me you're going to spend another night at home. I happen to know for a fact that there's no *Doctor Who* marathon on tonight, so you can bring your ass out with me and Tangela."

I could hear the thump of Young Jeezy in the background.

"This might come as a surprise to you, 'Keema, but I'm going out with a friend for drinks."

"Oh shit, my boy got a date. How long has it been?"

"You ain't got to remind me, and it's not a date, Ms. Nosy. We're just hangin' out for drinks."

"What's his name?"

"His name is Alan and that's all I'm telling you…for now."

"Alan…Alan. He sounds like a white boy."

"Not that it matters, but no he's not white. He's a brother."

"Well, go 'head then. I'm scared of you."

"Shakeema, I hate to cut this *riveting* conversation short, but I'm runnin' late."

"Call me tomorrow. I want to know all the dick-suckin' details."

Spoken like a true sailor at a biker bar.

"'Bye, girl. You and Tangela have fun tonight."

"We will, but I doubt we will have as much fun as you," Shakeema chortled.

By the time I got off the phone with Shakeema, it was seven-thirty. I grabbed my car keys and hauled ass. I figured I would get to the End Zone right at eight if not a few minutes before if I took shortcuts. My stomach was chockfull of butterflies, and my palms were sweaty.

The parking lot of the End Zone was packed with cars.

"Damn, they got valet parking tonight?" This blond-haired, college-age kid came around to the driver's side of my Buick. That was the first time I ever had someone park my car for me. It felt weird, but it was cool.

"Good evening, sir," he said.

I felt famous. He jumped into the front seat. It was weird seeing someone else other than me behind the wheel. I probably wouldn't have cared if he had stolen it. Shit is more trouble than it's worth. When I walked into the bar there were wall-to-wall bodies. Muffled chatter filled every corner and crevice of the swanky eatery. My heart was pounding out of control.

"Derrick!" I heard someone shout.

I looked past the crowd to find Alan's six-four, football-player frame sitting at one of the tables that was segregated from the crowd of barhoppers.

He was the finest man in the whole place as far as I was

concerned, dressed in faded, baggy jeans and a red Hollister T-shirt. "Hey," he said, gifting me with a smile.

"Man, this place is crazy. I didn't know it was going to be this packed on a Thursday night," I said.

I squeezed in between him and the table to get to the vacant seat. He smelled good as hell. I recognized the scent. Chrome, my favorite cologne next to Halston of course.

"It's ladies' night on Thursdays, so it's always full like this."

"What do you think?" Alan asked.

"It's pretty cool. I don't see a lot of young folks in here."

"That's why I chose this place. It's more of a mature, sophisticated kind of atmosphere. The grown folks got downtown while the young'uns can have the Tennessee Street Strip and Roxy's."

A voluptuous server with long, luxurious weave and big titties made her way over to us.

"My name is Kandee, and I will be your server this evening. Can I start you guys off with a drink?"

"I'll have a tall boy," Alan said.

"Let me get a vodka cranberry."

"All right. Here are your menus. I will be back shortly with your drinks."

"Thank you," said Alan.

We studied the menus.

"Get whatever you want. Dinner's on me."

I didn't want to order anything that was too pricey, like lobster or steak.

"So what time did you get here?" I asked.

"'Bout ten minutes before you."

"Yeah, sorry. My friend called me and wanted to chew my ear off."

"It's cool," Alan smiled. "I had to wait for a table to open up anyway."

"By the way, I ran into someone else from James Baldwin High today."

"Who?"

"You remember Jatari Booker?"

"Yeah, what's *he* up to?"

"He works at Tallahassee Capital Bank. He's divorced with two kids. He's got a townhouse over here in Blairstone Court."

"Nice."

"I ran into him at the mall with his daughter. He said that the twenty-year high school reunion is coming up. He asked me if I was going. I had totally forgotten about it until Jatari mentioned it."

"Seandra Milson told me about it. Remember her?"

"I bet she's still a kiss-ass."

"Probably so," Alan laughed, "but are you going to the reunion?"

Kandee returned with our drinks.

"You guys ready?"

"I'm going to get the charbroiled chicken sandwich," I said.

"You want regular or sweet-potato fries with that?"

"Sweet-potato fries."

"Would you like blue-cheese dressing?" the server asked.

"Yeah, blue cheese."

I live for blue cheese. I'll put it on just about anything.

Kandee then turned to Alan.

"And for you, sir?"

"That shrimp burger. How is it cooked?"

"You can get it deep fried or charbroiled It's seasoned and served on a toasted bun. It's real good."

"Let me try that then, charbroiled with sweet-potato fries."

"Sounds good."

Kandee took our menus and made her way back through the crowd toward the kitchen.

"What, and see people that made my life a living hell?" I took a sip from my vodka cranberry. "C'mon. Those people were *your* friends. They only liked me because I hung out with you."

"It wasn't all that bad was it?"

"I'm not gonna lie. Those parties were off the chain."

"And those assholes like Eldridge Jamison and Devon Blake stopped fuckin' with you when they saw that you were friends with the entire basketball team."

"I still got called faggot this and faggot that. The girls wanted to fuck you and the guys wanted to be you."

"And some of the guys wanted me to fuck them," Alan said.

I burst out laughing. Alan always knew when to crack a joke when shit was getting too serious. "You were the captain of the basketball team. Nobody was going to fuck with you."

"To be honest, it wasn't like I wanted to play ball."

"Oh shut up, whatever."

"No, seriously. My dad made me go out for the team. I got tired of his asshole friends asking me if I was going to go out for the team, telling me that my height and size was wasted if I wasn't either on the court or on a football field. My dad told me that I had to choose one or the other. Said he would take my car away if I didn't at least try out, and he is somebody you don't say no to," Alan said, taking a gulp from his glass of beer.

"Well, at least yours paid attention to you. Mine didn't care if I was passing or failing"

Kandee walked back over to our table.

"Would you like another beer?"

"Yes and another vodka cranberry for my friend here."

"Coming right up."

I was glad when her busty, big-titty behind left us alone.

"So did your dad have anything to do with you going into law enforcement?"

"That was my decision. He wanted me to go to college, but I wanted to go into the army, maybe make a career out of it."

"So what happened?"

"I got sick of it after about five years and decided to leave and come back home."

"Did you go to Iraq?"

"I was stationed in Afghanistan for about a year. You just wouldn't believe the shit that goes on over there. You realize just how lucky you are and how much we take for granted when you go to a country that doesn't have the same freedoms."

Kandee returned with Alan's beer and my vodka cranberry. "Your orders are almost ready."

This sista was working hard for the money.

"So you came back home—"

"I came home and decided to go into the police academy. I've wanted to be a cop ever since I was six years old. The military paid my way through. A friend of mine who works for TPD got me on."

"I couldn't be a cop."

"Why do you say that?"

"I'm not knockin' ya'll for what you do. It's just that ya'll see sides to people that nobody else sees. I would prefer to watch it all on TV."

Alan guffawed. "Well, don't believe everything you see on the boob tube. When you have seen what I have, dealing with stuff over here is a cakewalk."

I took a sip from my drink.

"Are you still writing?" Alan asked.

"I just finished the first draft of a novel."

"Damn, Derrick, that's great."

"We'll see if it turns out to be anything."

I noticed Kandee making her way back over to our table with a tray of food.

"Hold on here she comes."

"Charbroiled chicken with bacon." She sat my plate down in front of me. The sweet-potato fries were like eye candy to my stomach.

"Careful, baby. Those are hot," she said.

"And here's your shrimp burger. Can I get you guys anything else?"

"No, I think we're good," Alan said.

"Enjoy your meal and I will be back a little later to check on ya'll."

I poured the small cup of blue cheese on my chicken burger and sweet potato fries while Alan drowned his in ketchup.

"I remember seeing you sometimes writing in that purple notebook of yours."

"Acts of a budding writer," I said, before working a couple of fries in my mouth.

"So you're not the least bit interested to see how much weight Seandra and all them other chicks has gained, who got married, and who has a litter of kids?"

I laughed. "I don't know, man, maybe."

"Even if I asked you to go with me?"

"You mean like as your—"

"As my date, yeah."

"Damn, you're good."

"So I take that as a yes, you'll come? I would love to show up with a published writer on my arm," Alan said.

"If you're trying to flatter me, it's working."

The juices from the shrimp burger dripped from the corners of Alan's mouth. I wanted to reach over the table and use my tongue to sop it up. The way he was wolfing down his food, I knew he could put it down in the bedroom just as hard. (Pun damn well intended.) I thought of his lips being pressed up against mine. I pulled at my growing hard-on under the table.

"What?" Alan said.

"Nothing."

"Is there ketchup on my face?"

"No. I'm just...happy to be here that's all."

Alan glanced down shyly at his plate.

I felt all those feelings I'd had for him as a teenager reeling back.

"Well, I would much rather be here with you than out on the street, breathing in the drunken stench of some bum."

I noticed Kandee sauntering back over.

"Is everything all right over here?" How's that shrimp burger?"

"It's pretty good."

"I toldja. Well, let me know if ya'll need anything else."

My dick wouldn't ease up no matter how many times I kept pushing it down. Once it gets hard, it's got a mind of its own.

"Would you guys like some dessert? We got some cherry cobbler fresh out of the oven."

"As tempting as that sounds, I don't think we got room," I told her.

"All right, well here's your check and you guys have a nice night. Come back and see us."

"Thank you. It was a great meal," Alan said.

"So how 'bout a nightcap?" I asked.

Alan started laughing.

"What?" I grinned.

"People actually say that? Nightcap."

"Fuck you," I joked.

"Yeah, a *nightcap* sounds good," Alan said with a snide expression like he knew what was *really* up. He pulled his wallet out of the back pocket of his jeans.

Alan slid some large bills under the receipt.

I was scared to get up from the table with my dick hard against my crotch. I followed Alan through the mingling crowd.

"Have a nice night, guys," Kandee yelled, giving us one of those cutesy waves A-list actresses give on red carpet events.

As I followed Alan out of the congested restaurant, he reached his hand back to me. He hesitated for a couple seconds and then slid mine into his. My heart jumped when our hands interlocked. The cool, spring air kissed my face when we reached the exit of the bar and grill. People were still standing outside, waiting for tables or spots at the bar.

Alan handed the valet his ticket.

"We can take my car," Alan said.

"Will mine be okay here?"

"I'll let the valet know."

He whispered something in the young brotha's ear and slid him some money.

I slid into the black Expedition with smoke-gray leather seats.

"He says you should be fine. I'll bring you back in the morning to get your car."

"This is nice," I said, as I studied the inside of the SUV.

"But it kicks my ass in gas."

My dick had softened in my jeans by the time we got to Alan's crib, a posh townhouse on the north side.

"Damn, this is beautiful. You stay here by yourself?"

"Shit, on a rookie cop's salary? My roommate, Satoya, splits the mortgage. She's in Atlanta with some friends. She's better than my last roommate."

I made myself comfortable on the peanut-butter-tan sectional. "You want something to drink? I got soda, water, apple juice and some Stoli vodka Satoya got in here."

"Water is fine." I didn't want Alan to think that I needed to get drunk to be with him.

He joined me in the living room with bottled water and a beer for him. I was getting nervous. My palms were sweaty.

"I had a great night," Alan said.

"I did too. That was fun. I don't always get a chance to..."

Alan started to massage my chest. It had been a while since someone had touched me like that. He eased his hand under my shirt, sliding it up my stomach. I felt a finger traipse along my nipples. My dick was growing in my jeans again, and this time, I didn't give a damn. He started to kiss along my neck. When he nibbled the lobe of my left ear, I thought I was going to nut right there.

"You used to like it when I did this."

"I still do."

Alan sat our drinks on the coffee table in front of us. It was about to be on and popping. When I turned to him, our lips met and sent off sparks of lust that took me back to those after-school make-out sessions in his parents' living room. I could taste the beer on his tongue. He tugged me closer, leaning into me. He peeled off his shirt. Mine snagged on my glasses.

"Hold up," he laughed, helping me out of the purple Polo. Our skin kissed.

I thought of his dick bone-hard in his jeans.

Alan led me into his bedroom, which was immaculate. We

eased out of our jeans and shoes before we smeared ourselves onto his king-size bed. Our thick, chocolate dicks bobbed freely from our drawz, protruding from our rotund hips.

Alan wrapped his fingers around my dick, massaging my nine inches, caressing my low hangers. His touch was gentle for a big, brute of a cop.

He eased his husky brawn along mine until we kissed. Our dicks and balls rubbed hot together.

"I want to feel you inside me," I told him.

I turned over on my stomach.

I watched him pull open the drawer of one of his bedside tables to pull out a bottle of lube and a rubber. I'd thought he might pull out cuffs or something. Fuck, that would have been hot. He tore the wrapper open and looked at me like I was in for the fucking of my life, as he rolled the rubber past the head, down the shaft. Alan flicked open the tube and squeezed a line of the clear grease along his magic stick.

Straddling me with his legs, he eased me apart and squeezed some lube between my booty cheeks. It was a little cool going on, but nice. I gripped the pillow. I was ready for the primo deep-dicking Alan was about to put on me. I jerked as he slathered it along my ditch, from tailbone to balls. My dick was hot and hard.

"You okay?" he asked.

"Oh yeah." The bedsprings squeaked under our weight as he maneuvered himself on top of me. I spread my legs as I felt the blunt head of his greased dick graze my ass. I was ready to give him all of me.

Alan applied more pressure. I braced myself. I felt him slide in, fucking me. His breath was hot against my neck. I couldn't do anything. I was pinned down with muscle and brute cop-dick.

"Fuck yeah, get that ass."

It had been so long. All that dick filled me, stretched me.

Work it.

Tear it up.

Alan gave my nips tempered squeezes as he fucked.

Thrust.

In.

Out.

In.

Push. Fuck yeah.

My left leg slumped over the brink of the mattress.

Alan grabbed me by my hips and arched my ass up to his dick. He was balls-deep.

I sucked my teeth, lips tight.

He's got me where he wants me.

"Work that ass," I hollered. *Harder. Harder.* I eased myself on my side.

Alan reached between my thighs for my dick and started to beat me off. His fingers were greasy from the lube.

I turned to kiss him as he fucked me.

"I'm gonna come," he said.

We looked into each other's eyes as we orgasmed. My cum oozed over his knuckles onto the bed. Alan eased his dick out of my ass.

We kissed, holding each other in a sweaty, cum-sticky embrace.

I watched Alan fall asleep. There was nowhere else I wanted to be.

ABOUT THE
AUTHORS

GAVIN ATLAS is the author of the collection *The Boy Can't Help It* and can be reached at gavinatlas@gmail.com. For information on The Project to End Human Trafficking, see endhumantrafficking.org.

BEARMUFFIN's erotic stories have appeared in many gay magazines over the past twenty years. Now his fiction can be found in anthologies from Alyson, Bold Strokes and Cleis Press. He lives in San Diego and loves to travel up and down the California coast searching for grist for his literary mill.

MICHAEL BRACKEN's short fiction has been published in *Best Gay Romance 2010*, *Beautiful Boys*, *Biker Boys*, *Black Fire*, *Boy Fun*, *Boys Getting Ahead*, *Country Boys*, *Freshmen*, *The Handsome Prince*, *Homo Thugs*, *Hot Blood: Strange Bedfellows*, *The Mammoth Book of Best New Erotica 4*, *Men*, *Muscle Men*, *Teammates* and many others.

ERIC DEL CARLO's (ericdelcarlo.com) erotic fiction of all stripes has appeared with Ravenous Romance, Circlet Press, Cleis Press, Loose Id and most recently with Ellora's Cave, who published his gonzo science fiction novel *Elyria's Ecstasy*, cowritten with Amber Jayne. Eric also writes a great deal of mainstream sci-fi and fantasy.

MARTHA DAVIS (facebook.com/quixoticorchid) is an Atlanta-based writer of erotic romance and M/M fiction who wants to thank Corporals C. and G. for all the great behind-the-scenes cop tidbits.

LANDON DIXON's stories appear in the anthologies *Straight? Volume 2, Friction 7, Working Stiff, Sex by the Book, I Like It Like That, Boys Caught In The Act, Service With A Smile, Teammates, Boys Getting Ahead, Nerdvana, Homo Thugs, Black Fire, Ultimate Gay Erotica 2005, 2007, and 2008* and *Best Gay Erotica 2009*.

D. FOSTALOVE has been published in numerous anthologies, including *Black Fire, Brief Encounters* and *Afternoon Pleasures*. He is currently at work on a follow-up to his debut novel, *Unraveled: Sealed Lips, Clenched Fists*.

T. HITMAN is the nom-de-porn of a professional writer whose short fiction appeared in *Men, Freshmen* and *Torso*, among others. For five years, he also wrote the Unzipped Web Review column and contributed hundreds of feature articles and interviews on some of the hottest men in the gay porn industry.

D. K. JERNIGAN (KathleenTudor.com) grew up with a family full of cops, but she certainly never saw the kinky side of things!

D. K. has been published in *Spellbound* and *Fraternal Devotion*. Under her supersecret alternate identity, Kathleen Tudor, D. K. has dozens of stories with presses including HarperCollins, Cleis, Circlet, Xcite and more.

UK resident **ANDY MCGREGGOR** has published twelve gay erotic novellas to date. His first, *McGreggor and the Castle of Bareback Virgins,* is the first in an ongoing series involving the eponymous character, Andy McGreggor. Other works include a collection of short stories and two historical novellas, available on Amazon.com and Amazon.co.uk.

JOHNNY MURDOC (queeryoungcowboys.com) is a writer, designer and micro-publisher. He lives in Saint Louis with his partner. Murdoc cofounded Sex Positive Saint Louis with three awesome people. Together they create safe spaces for the discussion of sexuality.

GREGORY L. NORRIS (gregorylnorris.blogspot.com) is the author of numerous novels for Ravenous Romance (ravenousromance.com), *The Q Guide to Buffy the Vampire Slayer* (Alyson Books), the recent *The Fierce and Unforgiving Muse—Twenty-Six Tales From the Terrifying Mind of Gregory L. Norris* (EJP), and *13 Creature Features* (Reaser Brand Communications).

ROB ROSEN (therobrosen.com), author of the novels *Sparkle: The Queerest Book You'll Ever Love,* the Lambda Literary Award-nominated *Divas Las Vegas, Hot Lava, Southern Fried* and *Queerwolf,* has had short stories featured in more than 150 anthologies.

K. VALE (kimbervale.com) writes erotica of all stripes. As

K. Vale, she pens gay erotic romance. Under the name on her driver's license, she writes horror. Stalk her on Facebook and Twitter @KimberVale. Come for the sex. Stay for the story.

MAX VOS is a classically trained chef with over 30 years of food service experience. "Cooking English," a short story, was his first published work, and since then Ravenous Romance has published five more of his short stories. His first novel, *P.O.W.*, was released in 2013 with MLR Press. His second novel, *My Hero*, was a bestseller.

SALOME WILDE (salandtalerotica.com) has published diverse pansexual erotic fiction, most of it appearing in collections edited by Susie Bright, Rachel Kramer Bussel, Maxim Jakubowski and others. Her contemporary gay romance novella *After the First Taste of Love* (coauthored with Talon Rihai) is available from Storm Moon Press.

LOGAN ZACHARY (loganzacharydicklit.com) is the author of *Calendar Boys*, a collection of stories, and *Big Bad Wolf*, a werewolf story set in Northern Minnesota. His work can be found in *Hard Hats, Best Gay Erotica 2009, Surfer Boys, Obsessed, College Boys, Skater Boys, Brief Encounters, Biker Boys, Beach Bums* and *Rough Trade*.

ABOUT
THE EDITOR

SHANE ALLISON's editing career began with the bestselling gay erotic anthology *Hot Cops: Gay Erotic Stories,* which was one of his proudest moments. Since the birth of his first anthology, he has gone on to publish over a dozen gay erotica anthologies such as *Straight Guys: Gay Erotic Fantasies, Cruising: Gay Erotic Stories, Middle Men: Gay Erotic Three-somes, Frat Boys: Gay Erotic Stories, Brief Encounters: 69 Hot Gay Shorts, College Boys: Gay Erotic Stories, Hardworking Men: Gay Erotic Fiction, Hot Cops: Gay Erotic Fiction, Back-draft: Fireman Erotica* and *Afternoon Pleasures: Erotica for Gay Couples.* Shane Allison has appeared in five editions *of Best Gay Erotica, Best Black Gay Erotica* and *Zane's Z-Rated: Chocolate Flava 3.* His debut poetry collection, *Slut Machine* is out from Queer Mojo and his poem/memoir *I Remember* is out from Future Tense Books. Shane is at work on a novel and currently resides in Tallahassee, Florida.

More from Shane Allison

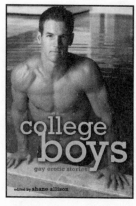

The Best in Gay Romance

Best Gay Romance 2014
Edited by Timothy Lambert and R. D. Cochrane

The best part of romance is what might happen next...that pivotal moment where we stop and realize, *This is wonderful.* But most of all, love—whether new or lifelong—creates endless possibilities. *Best Gay Romance 2014* reminds us all of how love changes us for the better.
ISBN 978-1-62778-011-7 $15.95

The Handsome Prince
Gay Erotic Romance
Edited by Neil Plàkcy

In this one and only gay erotic fairy tale anthology, your prince will come—and come again!
ISBN 978-1-57344-659-4 $14.95

Afternoon Pleasures
Erotica for Gay Couples
Edited by Shane Allison

Filled with romance, passion and lots of lust, *Afternoon Pleasures* is irresistibly erotic yet celebrates the coming together of souls as well as bodies.
ISBN 978-1-57344-658-7 $14.95

Fool for Love
New Gay Fiction
Edited by Timothy Lambert and R. D. Cochrane

For anyone who believes that love has left the building, here is an exhilarating collection of new gay fiction designed to reignite your belief in the power of romance.
ISBN 978-1-57344-339-5 $14.95

Boy Crazy
Coming Out Erotica
Edited by Richard Labonté

Editor Richard Labonté's unique collection of coming-out tales celebrates first-time lust, first-time falling into bed, and first discovery of love.
ISBN 978-1-57344-351-7 $14.95

Men on the Make

Wild Boys
Gay Erotic Fiction
Edited by Richard Labonté

Take a walk on the wild side with these fierce tales of
rough trade. Defy the rules and succumb to the charms of
hustlers, jocks, kinky tricks, smart-asses, con men, straight
guys and gutter punks who give as good as they get.
ISBN 978-1-57344-824-6 $15.95

Sexy Sailors
Gay Erotic Stories
Edited by Neil Plakcy

Award-winning editor Neil Plakcy has
collected bold stories of naughty, nautical
hunks and wild, stormy sex that are sure to
blow your imagination.
ISBN 978-1-57344-822-2 $15.95

Hot Daddies
Gay Erotic Fiction
Edited by Richard Labonté

From burly bears and hunky father figures
to dominant leathermen, *Hot Daddies* cap-
tures the erotic dynamic between younger
and older men: intense connections, con-
sensual submission, and the toughest and
tenderest of teaching and learning.
ISBN 978-1-57344-712-6 $14.95

Straight Guys
Gay Erotic Fantasies
Edited by Shane Allison

Gaybie Award-winner Shane Allison shares
true and we-wish-they-were-true stories in
his bold collection. From a husband on the
down low to a muscle-bound footballer,
from a special operations airman to a redneck daddy, these men will sweep you off
your feet.
ISBN 978-1-57344-816-1 $15.95

Cruising
Gay Erotic Stories
Edited by Shane Allison

Homemade glory holes in a stall wall,
steamy shower trysts, truck stop rendezvous...According to Shane Allison, "There's
nothing that gets the adrenaline flowing
and the muscle throbbing like public sex."
ISBN 978-1-57344-795-7 $14.95

Rousing, Arousing
Adventures with Hot Hunks

Best Erotica Series

"Gets racier every year."—*San Francisco Bay Guardian*

Best Women's Erotica 2014
Edited by Violet Blue
ISBN 978-1-62778-003-2 $15.95

Best Women's Erotica 2013
Edited by Violet Blue
ISBN 978-1-57344-898-7 $15.95

Best Women's Erotica 2012
Edited by Violet Blue
ISBN 978-1-57344-755-3 $15.95

Best Bondage Erotica 2014
Edited by Rachel Kramer Bussell
ISBN 978-1-62778-012-4 $15.95

Best Bondage Erotica 2013
Edited by Rachel Kramer Bussel
ISBN 978-1-57344-897-0 $15.95

Best Bondage Erotica 2012
Edited by Rachel Kramer Bussel
ISBN 978-1-57344-754-6 $15.95

Best Lesbian Erotica 2014
Edited by Kathleen Warnock
ISBN 978-1-62778-002-5 $15.95

Best Lesbian Erotica 2013
Edited by Kathleen Warnock
Selected and introduced by
Jewelle Gomez
ISBN 978-1-57344-896-3 $15.95

Best Lesbian Erotica 2012
Edited by Kathleen Warnock
Selected and introduced by
Sinclair Sexsmith
ISBN 978-1-57344-752-2 $15.95

Best Gay Erotica 2014
Edited by Larry Duplechan
Selected and introduced by Joe Manetti
ISBN 978-1-62778-001-8 $15.95

Best Gay Erotica 2013
Edited by Richard Labonté
Selected and introduced by Paul Russell
ISBN 978-1-57344-895-6 $15.95

Best Gay Erotica 2012
Edited by Richard Labonté
Selected and introduced by
Larry Duplechan
ISBN 978-1-57344-753-9 $15.95

Best Fetish Erotica
Edited by Cara Bruce
ISBN 978-1-57344-355-5 $15.95

Best Bisexual Women's Erotica
Edited by Cara Bruce
ISBN 978-1-57344-320-3 $15.95

Best Lesbian Bondage Erotica
Edited by Tristan Taormino
ISBN 978-1-57344-287-9 $16.95

Ordering is easy! Call us toll free or fax us to place your MC/VISA order.
You can also mail the order form below with payment to:
Cleis Press, 2246 Sixth St., Berkeley, CA 94710.

ORDER FORM

QTY	TITLE	PRICE

SUBTOTAL _____

SHIPPING _____

SALES TAX _____

TOTAL _____

Add $3.95 postage/handling for the first book ordered and $1.00 for each additional book. Outside North America, please contact us for shipping rates. California residents add 9% sales tax. Payment in U.S. dollars only.

★ Free book of equal or lesser value. Shipping and applicable sales tax extra.

Cleis Press • Phone: (800) 780-2279 • Fax: (510) 845-8001
orders@cleispress.com • www.cleispress.com
You'll find more great books on our website

Follow us on Twitter @cleispress • Friend/fan us on Facebook